LUCKY STAR

CHAPTER ONE

Tabitha had gone to sleep last night, actually looking forward to going back to the office after her holiday. She'd been keen to get the chance to show off her tan and be everybody's hero by providing sweets. The kind of sweets that were always appreciated more because they had travelled through a passport control desk so were obviously infinitely yummier than any other sweets. She'd anticipated dreamy talk over tea breaks of lazy sunny days and romantic nights, filled with music and dancing.

This morning though, she stared at her clock with contempt and disbelief. How could it possibly be time to get up when it was still dark outside? Life just wasn't fair. Sure, she'd just had ten beautiful days in Greece with the man of her dreams, but now it wasn't fair. Ok, so he had insisted on paying for everything as other girls had swooned over him as they passed by them, but still…right now…life was decidedly not darn fair.

Tabitha reached over to her bedside drawers and fumbled around for her glasses and mobile phone. If she checked her messages before getting up, maybe this would be her lucky day. There could always be that much prayed for instruction to not come to the office today as, "it's closed due to structural damage from an earth tremor", or "the buses aren't running due to heavy snow so please feel free to work from home", or even, "aliens have invaded……"

One message received. Could it be…aliens…? No! Just a reminder that her dental check-up was due. With a huff, Tabitha sat up and stretched. Her cat, Snuggles, looked over from his bed in the corner of the room and added insult to injury by curling up into a neat ball and heading back contentedly to the land of nod. Tabitha looked at the clock again which seemed to be moving on dramatically quickly. There was nothing for it. With the aliens having apparently failed her once again, she was just going to have to get moving.

A shower and two strong coffees later, Tabitha felt a little more human as she looked in her almost bare food cupboards. She was definitely going to need to go shopping after work or maybe, brainwave gratefully received, she could invite herself to Mum's for dinner in order to put the supermarket off for another day.

After firing off an unashamed begging text, she was pleased to receive a message back from her Mum immediately saying that she'd love her to come over. The phone pinged again and Mum added that she was cooking braising steak. Bonus. It was one of the things that Tabitha could never be bothered to cook for herself. Another message let her know that George, Tabitha's brother, was also due round. That's a right result, she thought as she popped their souvenirs into her handbag. Maybe today did have the potential to be bearable after all.

The bus turned up the very second she arrived at her stop so yes, that was also a good sign that today would be alright, she concluded. Tabitha was strongly into signs although she did acknowledge that quite often she would actually be manipulating something into being a sign for what she wanted to believe was going to happen. A solo Magpie, however, could make her wary for an entire day though, occasionally leading to it being a day of calamity, purely because of her constant trepidation.

She gazed out of the window with fondness now as the bus travelled around her hometown. She found that she always looked at everything just a little bit differently after being away, almost retaining her tourist's eye. Old buildings, that she would often take for granted, now stood out to her as the beautiful artistic structures that they deserved to be appreciated as.

She took in the changing colours of the leaves adorning old familiar trees, the early morning mist blanketing the park and the rising sun spreading a glorious red tint across it all. It wasn't quite so bad to be back home after all.

By the time she walked into the offices of Perfect Promos she was excited to see everybody again. She reminded herself too that, despite feeling like she had gained a few little holiday wobbly bits, her fabulous golden glow did deserve to be celebrated.

She didn't think of herself as a particularly vain person. She couldn't be doing with the effort of false lashes and tattooed eyebrows and all that rigmarole but what girl doesn't like a 'great tan' compliment every now and again.

Tabitha's colleagues were suitably awesome, actually surpassing the hoped for appreciation of her bronzeness as they swarmed around her desk to partake in her sugary souvenirs and welcome her home. She quickly got back into the swing of being at work and was soon reminded of the buzz that her job provided her with.

Tabitha had ended up working in advertising quite by accident. She had finished school with some examinations in the basic office skills as, failing any specific career yearnings, it seemed like the sensible course to take.

However, secretarial roles had become few and far between as technology had become more advanced. Ironically, she had been a whizz at Shorthand just as it seemed that companies were all switching to dictaphones. So she had been left without a clue of what she was going to do as school came to an end and the school's careers officer also seemed to be struggling to keep up with the transition in the workplaces from people to computers.

As Tabitha and her friends had signed each other's school shirts on the last day of term, whilst pledging through their tears that they would keep in touch forever, she couldn't believe that it was actually time to be a grown up for real.

After a mad panic she had found herself working at a children's trampolining club. It was so much fun that it hadn't actually felt like work but she knew that she couldn't stay there forever and actually earn enough money to, one day, move out from the family home. Reluctantly, she had torn herself away and started to look for what she supposed would be a 'proper job'.

She had responded to Perfect Promos' advertisement for a short term temp, required to set up a new filing system. It was only for a couple of weeks but she decided that it would at least make her CV begin to look a little more professional. It transpired though that this was where she was meant to be as the company had kept finding reasons to keep her on longer, eventually making her a junior member of the advertising team. She had been here now for approaching six years and was involved in training up the new juniors as well as having acquired her own portfolio of customers.

She loved that she earned a living from basically thinking up eye-catching and occasionally completely wacky ideas. She also got to work with a wide variety of companies, ranging from huge pension providers to the local toy shop. She had often laughed at adverts on the tv and wondered how on earth the creator had come up with the concept. It excited her to think that some of the most famous adverts may have begun with somebody saying, "What about if…?" Now she was that person, having obscure lightbulb moments in the middle of the night that often became something tangible to work with.

Tabitha spent the next few hours trawling through her emails and catching up on everything that had happened while she was away. Time flew by and it was only her tummy grumbling indignantly that reminded her that she should actually take a break for some lunch.

She headed outside and plopped herself down on the grass next to the river. Another benefit of working where she did was having this beautiful setting just a five minute walk from her desk. Alas, the sun had hidden itself away now behind thick layers of low cloud and Tabitha questioned whether her choice of a mid-length linen skirt to show off her tanned legs had been a good one. She wasn't certain that goose pimples were a great look for her.

Or for anybody really for that matter. She also noted that she needed to moisturise again when she went back inside if her golden colour was going to last.

She waved cheerily at a narrowboat pootling past. A gorgeous black Labrador in a life jacket wagged it's tail excitedly as it's owners waved back at her. A pair of geese rode the gentle waves that had been created by the boat, honking noisily as they passed by.

Being back in her own dear country certainly provided some delights for sure. Now that she was away from her desk though, she realised that the feeling in her tummy wasn't just hunger. She suddenly became aware that she was suffering with a case of withdrawals due to being away from her wonderful man. She had, after all, gotten used to spending every minute with him. Gary was now back at his home, twenty miles away which felt like a whole world away right now. Tabitha pulled out her phone and typed a quick message to him.

Hey sweetie. Hope you're doing ok. I'm missing your face! Looking forward to seeing you at the weekend xxx

She hoped that he would be able to write straight back or even call so that she could hear his voice but decided after a while that he must be busy at work or possibly driving. She ate her avocado and marmite on crispbread, an attempt at regaining her pre-holiday flattish tummy and shook the leftover crumbs onto the grass for the birds.

She was feeling comfy on the grass and contemplated how nice a quick afternoon nap would be. The chill in the air certainly confirmed that she was no longer on holiday though and there would be no nap today. As she headed back indoors she was grateful for the warmth of the lift and she made a mental note to dig out her longer skirts for the fast approaching end of summer.

CHAPTER TWO

As Tabitha walked into her Mum's front garden that evening, the door was flung wide open. Her Mum hugged her like she hadn't seen her for months. "Oh darling, you look great. You have indeed been kissed by the sun." She continued to look her up and down, assessing her offspring. "You need to keep moisturising now though. I reckon I've just taken some of your tan off simply by hugging you."

"Thanks Mum, I know, I've been moisturising all..."

"Come in, come in love. I need to check the oven quick. George is out the back with Scott if you want to go and say hi."

Tabitha popped her bag down and wandered out into the back garden where her brother and his sidekick were sitting vaping. A smell of Vanilla filled the air and the vape smoke seemed limitless.

"Yo bro. Good to see you old boy." Tabitha thoroughly enjoyed taking the mickey out of her brother for being older than her, albeit only two years despite not liking it when he laughed at her for being younger. She did acknowledge that she was beyond help at times. "Wow, that is some contraption you've got there George. Pleased to see you're still off the fags."

"Hey Sis. Cheers, how's it going?" George held out a hand for a fist pump then, pleasantries over, added "That tan looks fake to me I reckon. What do you think Scott?"

Tabitha gently slapped her brother round the head as Scott smiled politely at her. "It looks like a proper tan to me. It suits you Tabby."

"Thanks Scott. At least there are some gentlemen around here."

Scott responded with his usual blush and Tabitha smiled fondly. He was definitely her favourite out of her brother's group of friends. She guessed he wasn't all that comfortable conversing with the female of the species though as he was a man of few words whenever she was about. Maybe one day she would have to help him to find a nice young lady.

"Dinner's ready kids. Grab it while it's hot", Mum called out from the kitchen and the three of them bundled indoors like puppies in need of feeding.

Tabitha's Mum wanted to know everything about the holiday so no details were spared, down to the specifics of which restaurants had offered a set menu and how many hours of sunbathing had been attained each day.

"Oh Mum. It was such a marvellous place, everyone was so friendly and Gary was just wonderful and the nights were so dreamy."

The boys shared a look of revulsion that they were having to be party to this atrocious discussion, especially over their dinner.

"See boys." Tabitha's Mum turned to them both. "If you didn't fritter all your earnings away on pubs, takeaways and horses you could have nice holidays too. George, you need to take a leaf out of your sister's book and save some money for something nice."

It was Tabitha's turn to blush as she recollected how Gary had hardly let her put her hand in her own purse at all. He must really care about her to want to spoil her so much.

George laughed at his Mum's advice. "We are saving money Mum, we're eating here init? Exactly the same as golden balls over there." He poked his tongue out at Tabitha. "Anyway we work really hard. We've got to have some fun. Life is proper tough for our generation." He gave his Mum a wink, hinting that he was just trying to wind her up a bit.

Tabitha and Scott both grinned at George's declaration. Tabitha's Mum shook her head in dismay, realising that she didn't stand a chance if the three of them were now in cahoots. "You lot are a pain in my posterior and you are now in charge of washing up after dinner." Tabitha and George glared at each other across the table, each blaming the other for having now acquired chores when they didn't even live here anymore. The family shenanigans were, however, a welcome and amusing distraction from missing Gary.

She and Gary had been dating for over a year now and he seemed to have enjoyed spoiling her more and more during the last few months. Sometimes though she wished that he would just send a quick hello message now and again, even if he was too busy to chat properly.

Their first meeting had been like a comedy scene from a soppy film or one of those chick lit novels where anything goes. The ones where the author feels like they can write whatever they want and we'll sit and obligingly picture the scene.

So..It had been a beautiful sunny day. The kind where everybody you meet on your travels greets you warmly and life just seems to stand still a little as families spend time together, picnicking and throwing frisbees . Even the birds seemed to whistle their hellos and the flowers danced merrily in a welcomed slight breeze....

Whilst jogging in the park, Tabitha's attention had become focused on a huge kite that had been circling above her head for a while now and seemed to be getting increasingly closer. She'd wondered if it could tell how exhausted she was feeling and she had gradually become more and more certain that it was preparing to swoop down to feed on her, the very moment she collapsed.

She had quickened her pace in an effort to look tough to her predator as she'd anxiously wiped her brow, thus causing her MP3 player to fly out of her pocket. Thankfully, the wire hadn't been long enough to trip her but her overlooked loose shoelace sure was. She'd gone down in slow motion in a chaotic jumble of arms, legs, wires and laces.

Thank goodness nobody had seen her...or maybe....Oh balls! The bugger of a universe had chosen that precise moment to introduce Gary Saunders into her life. It turned out that he didn't even live that close by, but destiny decided that his awareness of her existence was imperative at that very nanosecond, on that very day as she'd laid sprawled in a defeated heap by the side of the running track.

After helping her to hobble home, Tabitha had been quite sure that she wouldn't see Gary again. She must have looked like such a nincompoop.

Later that evening she'd cringed as she pictured the scene over and over in her head and somehow managed to look dafter every time. He had phoned though, as promised, to see how she was and they had ended up chatting for ages and had, since that day, embarked on the most wonderful romance in the universe ever, even upstaging the romances in the best hollywood films, ever

ever ever amen. Tabitha would sometimes get a little carried away when she thought about Gary.

It was a shame though that he hadn't managed to write back to her since she'd sent her message at lunchtime today. She supposed that he must have a lot of work to catch up on after their holiday. He'd message later or maybe tomorrow for sure.

Back at home that night, Tabitha was mournfully packing away her bikinis when her phone finally pinged. She typed in her pin excitedly and strained her eyes to see the screen, expecting Gary to be adorably apologetic for taking so long to reply to her.

Instead though, a message from her best friend, Pam popped up.

Hey Tabs. Welcome home. I thought I'd give you a chance for your holiday comedown to pass. I don't want no grumpy chat. Ha ha. Are you coming down The Shetlands on Friday?

Gonna be a lot of people out cos it's payday. Missed you babe xx

Tabitha was keen to catch up with her pals but she wasn't sure yet when Gary would want to see her. If he was seeing his friends this weekend, she would need to fit some time in around his plans.

Hey Pammy darling. Thanks for messaging. Sorry, but can I let you know later in the week if I can make it? I may be seeing Gary. Missed you loads xx

Her screen lit up again immediately

Ah boo to that. He's just stolen you away from us for too long already. Let me know when you know hon. Maybe Gary can come out with us too?! xx

That would be a perfect solution, Tabitha thought, but Gary didn't really like her local pub. She wondered if Pam really wanted him to come out anyway or if maybe she knew that he could be a little bit 'judgy' and was making a subtle point.

Gary thought that The Shetlands pub was 'a tad loud' and that some of her friends were 'a little squawky' when they were drunk. Tabitha actually thought that being 'a little squawky' was a good side effect of people having fun, but nevertheless, she didn't want to put him through it if it wasn't a comfortable situation for him.

Tabitha was just nodding off when her phone pinged and Gary's name finally flashed up on the screen.

Hi, Sorry it's so late. Things have been crazy busy. I'm heading to Brighton on Saturday morning for the weekend but maybe I could come over after work on Friday and crash at yours? My journey will be shorter the next day then and of course I get to see you! I'll see you 6ish babe xx

Tabitha was relieved that she had a plan to see him but also felt sad to let her friends down. Maybe she could catch up with them on Saturday night if they were about but she had a feeling that Pam would certainly not be thrilled when she told her that Gary had asked/advised her he would be coming over on Friday but what could she do?

She smiled giddily at the screensaver picture on her phone of her and Gary, dressed to the nines and smiling blissfully on their last night in Greece. It was one of her favourite shots from the holiday as she had decided that it looked almost like an engagement photo.

She wondered when they would get engaged, how and where would he ask her? Would he speak to her Mum first? Mum would like that. She fell off to sleep picturing the scene of her bashfully showing off her sparkling rock to everybody. "Oh it's nothing", she would say. "Oh we really didn't expect such a fuss" and, "Oh my, all these gifts, how sweet".

CHAPTER THREE

Friday finally arrived but it seemed to last forever. Tabitha had repeatedly found herself daydreaming at her desk. She blinked her eyes, bringing herself back to the room, trying to stop herself from picturing Gary's smile, his smell, his shoulders, his chest, mmm....She was grateful to be saved from becoming a mesmerised jelly a few times by her phone ringing. She definitely needed the distraction of her customers today as her emotions had even managed to stop her from eating her lunch.

As 6pm finally arrived, Tabitha sat down at the dining room table and filled two large glasses with wine, ready for Gary's impending arrival. She had already drunk one glass in a bid to curb her excitement and was feeling slightly fuzzy after her lack of appetite for food earlier. She had decided to attempt to recreate a night from their holiday and their starters of feta and olive salad looked amazing in the candlelight, if she did say so herself.

She had curled her long brown hair into beachy waves and she wore a fitted red dress which had required her to undertake some quick sit ups. Tabitha's first ever attempt at a from scratch Moussaka had been prepped and was ready to be popped into the oven as soon as Gary arrived. She had failed to track down any Ouzo in time but that was probably for the best. She wasn't as good at drinking as she occasionally thought she was.

Tabitha clicked into Facebook to see what everyone else was up to and grinned at her friends at the pub along the road, already looking quite merry after just over an hour. Pam always got rosy cheeks after just one drink though, to be fair, making her look drunker than she usually was. She could see that their friend, Laura was there too. Laura had two young kids so didn't get to come out with them that often at the moment so Tabitha was disappointed that she would be missing her this evening. Tonight would be wonderful though. She had some romantic music cued up and she was hoping that her and Gary could escape straight back to where they had left off on their beautiful holiday.

When the time got to 6:20pm, Tabitha began to get a little concerned. Gary was usually very good with his punctuality. She checked the traffic online and the rush hour all seemed to have cleared between them. She could text him but if he was driving she shouldn't distract him. If he was packing for his weekend away, she supposed that he may have lost track of time a little. She was sure that he'd be here soon.

She decided that she had better put the Moussaka in the oven now as it being half cooked for too long could potentially end up giving them both food poisoning. They would just have to swap their courses round. She put cling film over the salads and popped them away in the fridge. As she was now halfway down her second glass of wine she took another bottle out of the cupboard and put it on the table, ready for later.

She skimmed through the latest entertainment news on her phone, feeling slightly envious of the celebs that were frolicking around in the sea and clinking their champagne glasses gleefully. She had clicked into a newspaper's website that she found totally godawful, but unfortunately, to her shame, it occasionally lured her in by providing the best showbiz gossip. Tabitha squinted to try to recognise a reality star who she had momentarily muddled up with somebody else. She wished they wouldn't put so much filler in their lips. In her opinion they all looked better before having work done and, of course, it made it harder to work out who was who. The thought reminded her though to reapply her own lipstick which was now mostly adorning the rim of her wine glass.

It was now 6:40pm and still no sign. Tabitha refilled her glass again, promising herself that she would wait until Gary arrived to drink this one. She poured herself some tap water and felt disappointed that, despite the sensible notion, the pint glass ('borrowed' from The Shetlands) made her table display look a little less classy.

As the clock approached 7pm, Tabitha managed to convince herself that she must have got the plan wrong.

She must have read Gary's message incorrectly. Maybe he was actually due at 7pm and any time now the front doorbell would ring.

She half jumped out of her seat as the silence was suddenly broken by the oven timer going off and her phone pinging at the same time. She grabbed her phone and was relieved to see Gary's name pop up on the screen. She frantically tapped into his message.

Hi babe. Sorry, I won't be able to come over tonight after all. Something has come up and it's just gonna get too late. Hope it's not too much trouble. Will catch up next week xx

Tabitha felt hot tears of disappointment spring into her eyes. She wasn't usually much of a crier but she had made so much effort and was so looking forward to seeing him at last. The wine probably had an assist too and the tears now flowed uncontrollably down her cheeks.

She went to the mirror in the living room and carefully removed her contact lenses as they threatened to remove themselves and slumped onto the sofa, folding her arms around herself to try to regain her composure. She told herself that she was being silly and thought how sad Gary would be if he saw how upset she was. She then began to feel guilty about Gary being sad at her sadness and cried even more.

Eventually, it seemed that she had run out of tears and she let out a hiccup as a final sob got caught in her throat. Well she may as well get herself comfy now. After all, nobody wears a red dress with no company.

She felt a little more stable by the time that she had changed into her baggy joggers and a Rolling Stones t-shirt. And at least she had more wine and... "Oh Moussaka. Darn it", she squealed, running back out to the kitchen. As she opened the oven door, the smell of heavenly, albeit positively charred, moussaka spread around the kitchen. She carefully placed the dish on the cooker and looked through the drawers for a suitable ladle. Tipsy inspiration struck though and, deciding that she could save on washing up and effort, she put the Moussaka straight on to the table and spooned the delicious food straight from the dish into her mouth, remembering that, to be fair, she had skipped lunch.

She wondered momentarily if she could go and meet her friends after all, but decided that she had probably drank too much wine already to make a respectable entrance. She was also both highly embarrassed about being stood up and was now ironically underdressed.

An entire Moussaka later, Tabitha curled up on the sofa with more wine and watched Dirty Dancing for about the hundredth time on her own.

CHAPTER FOUR

Tabitha slept in late the next day until she was eventually woken by the sound of the front door bell ringing. She peered out of her bedroom window to see the edge of a huge bouquet of flowers poking out from under the porch. She raced down the stairs, quicker than she should have been able to, joyful that apparently Gary hadn't gone on his trip after all. He was obviously going to make it up to her for last night and wanted to surprise her.

However, as she pulled the front door wide open, she came face to face with a lady in a blinding bright orange uniform paired with a bright, beaming smile. Tabitha pulled her dressing gown around her tightly and tried not to look too disappointed.

"Good morning", her surprise caller exclaimed enthusiastically, obviously unaware of Tabitha's rather delicate condition. "Are you Tabitha?" She nodded in response to her own question before Tabitha could open her mouth to respond. "If so, I am here to deliver these to you. Happy Saturday!" She thrust the flowers out to her dramatically.

Tabitha accepted the huge bouquet and pulled the message card out, squinting to read the message.

Sorry about last night darling, I hope this makes it better

xx

She smiled at the eager delivery lady. "Wow, they're beautiful, thank you very much. Have a good day."

Her keen visitor wasn't in a rush to leave though and she shuffled from foot to foot as she waited to see if any juicy information was forthcoming. "So, are they from a young man? You're a lucky girl, they're from our most expensive range. I'm not supposed to say that." The delivery lady tapped the side of her nose and gave a wink as she disclosed this information.

"Yes they are from my boyfriend, thank you. I am lucky indeed. Bye now."

Tabitha closed the door slowly, trying not to seem rude. She was not really appreciating the bright sunshine that felt like it was lasering her eyes after her wine intake last night.

Thankfully the flowers were already in their own receptacle as she didn't think she owned a vase big enough for Gary's apology bouquet. She placed them on the lounge table and dialled Gary's phone number to thank him but the call went straight through to his voicemail. He must be on his way to Brighton now then, she guessed.

Tabitha looked in the fridge to see what could potentially fix her hangover. Two feta and olive salads rubbed in the fact that she had been stood up last night but at least they would be a reasonably healthier hangover cure than the bacon sandwich that she had been contemplating.

She poured herself some orange juice and picked at one of the salads whilst skimming through Facebook. She liked the pictures of Pam and the girls, prompting her phone to ping immediately. Pam's name popped up.

Hey hon. Hope you two had a lovely night. If you're free for the rest of the weekend, I'm up for going out again tonight if you want to. Just shout me. Dying to see you xx

Thank goodness, thought Tabitha, with the total confirmation that she was indeed a lucky girl. Not only had

Gary been amazing enough to send her flowers, her friends were completely awesome too. It would have been far too easy to have skulked around lazily all weekend but now she could still catch up with everybody.

Either a jog or a nap was going to be needed to clear the cobwebs away in preparation for going out though. After a quick toss up between the two, she took her breakfast up to her bedroom and crawled back under the duvet.

When Tabitha walked up to the pub that evening, she was surprised to find Pam sitting outside with George and Scott in tow.

Pam jumped up and ran over to greet her friend, looking her up and down enviously.

"Well I had thought that your tan would have faded by now, you ratbag. Get out of here. I may just hang with your lovely brother instead."

Tabitha laughed at her brother being called lovely but noted that he actually looked pretty chuffed with the compliment. She put her jacket down next to Scott and asked who would like a drink.

"Good timing, all of us please Sis", laughed George. "Here you go, you can keep the change."

Tabitha looked at the twenty pound note and decided that it was a fair exchange for going in to the bar when she had been planning to go in there anyway. When she returned with the tray of drinks, Pam and George were looking at his phone together. George was explaining something to her quite fervently.

"So you see, just cos that horse's latest finishing positions are 2 1 1 2, it doesn't automatically reflect how well it'll do tomorrow. You have to take the condition of the ground into account. Some prefer it soft and some prefer it hard."

Pam giggled naughtily. Tabitha peered over her glasses at the two of them. They had obviously known each other for a long time but something seemed different. They were sat very closely together, looking at the phone and George had a smart shirt on. Wow, how long had she actually been away for, she pondered to herself.

"What are you boys up to then?" Tabitha probed, feeling increasingly suspicious of their presence.

"Not a lot Sis", replied George, matter of factly.

"We're off to the races at Newbury tomorrow so we're just out for a couple tonight. Thought we might as well stay local." Scott helpfully gave a more informative answer, apparently feeling more confident to chat after a beer.

"Ah fun. We should do that sometime Pam. You know, the races. Maybe we could have a little splutter."

The group fell about laughing.

Scott put his hand gently on her arm. "I think you mean a flutter, Tabby."

He looked down and removed his hand, blushing slightly now, the colour flowing down his neck into his t-shirt. He picked up his beer and looked off into the distance.

"Sooo", exclaimed Pam. "How was your night of passion and romance? Worth missing a wild night down here for?"

"Oh for goodness sake Pamela", exclaimed George. "That's my sister. My ears can't take any more of their cute crap."

Tabitha shrugged. "Don't worry bro. I got well and truly stood up. Dinner for two was eaten by one." She patted her tummy. "It's ok though. Gary has been working ever so hard and is really busy after the holiday. He sent some lovely fuchsias to apologise."

"Fuchsias smoochias", muttered Scott. "Well, that's ok then."

They all looked at Scott, surprised by his untypical outburst. He looked rather shocked himself and he quickly pulled a silly face. "Ha ha, did I sound serious or what then?"

Tabitha was glad that Scott's joke had lightened the mood at least and she moved to change the subject quickly. She didn't totally feel that she could defend Gary convincingly when she was still feeling a little sore about the situation herself.

"So anyway Pam, What have I missed while I was away?" She was certain that Pam and the boys exchanged a look before Pam began to impart gossip about what their other friends had been up to in the past couple of weeks.

As she was speaking though, Tabitha began to feel as though there was a bit of a surreal atmosphere, almost as if she was looking in from outside but she put it down to her hangover. Could you have beer-fear if you had drank wine?, she wondered. Wine-whine? No, that was silly. Vino red-dread. Ooh that was better but she would continue to work on it when she wasn't in company.

George and Scott stuck to their word and made an early exit from the pub, in preparation for their horse racing meeting the next day. George surprised her by planting a kiss on top of her head.

"Get home safe sis. Try to be good." Then he walked back round the table and bent and kissed Pam on the head too. "You too Pamela dear."

Tabitha stared with her mouth open until her brother and Scott were safely out of earshot.

"Have I missed something? What's with you two weirdos?"

"What are you talking about hon?" Pam shook her head dismissively. "I just missed you, so it was nice to have another Morris around to make me laugh. That's all. Now let's go in. It's getting proper chilly out here."

With that Pam stood up and sloped off casually into the pub, putting an immediate end to the conversation.

CHAPTER FIVE

Gary continued to be elusive until Tuesday when he finally called. Tabitha couldn't believe that they had now gone as long without seeing each other as they had just spent together on holiday.

"Sweetie, I know that work is crazy busy but I really miss you", she admitted.

"I'm sorry babe. Everything's just non-stop at the moment. I'll make it up to you, ok? You're still good to come to the Brinkley function on Saturday aren't you?"

"Oh yeah, of course", agreed Tabitha, although she wasn't sure that he had actually mentioned it previously. "Remind me what time you need me to be ready for?"

The Brinkley's annual garden party last year had been their first big public event as an official couple. Tabitha remembered how nervous she had felt, schmoozing with all the big wigs including customers of Gary's company. They had all been absolutely charming though and had made her feel very welcome and included, as the girlfriend of the up and coming hot shot investor.

"I'll pick you up at 1pm. Oh and maybe wear that red dress you wore on holiday. That looked stunning on you."

"Ah ok, I will, thanks", she responded, pleased that Gary couldn't see her as her hand flew to her forehead in disbelief.

Tabitha didn't know whether to laugh or cry when she got off the phone. Great, the red dress. The one that she'd been wearing on Friday night when Gary had been a no show to her awesome dinner. The one with mascara and potentially snot on the sleeve. The one that she would now have to get dry cleaned pretty quickly. Oh well, at least she knew that he would have liked it if he had made it round last Friday.

She glanced at her hair in the mirror. She could probably do with a bit of a trim too. The gorgeous Greek weather had played havoc in creating some rather fluffy ends.

She quickly wrote herself a note to book in for a hair appointment and go to the dry cleaners sometime this week. She needed to make a big effort for Gary as this was a huge event for his and, therefore, their future.

The following Saturday, Tabitha was thankful for the effort that she had made as Gary led her into the beautiful gardens of the Brinkley estate. She was aware of heads turning as they walked along. Gary looked dashing in a suit which she imagined had probably been purchased especially for today and he smelt divine. It had taken all of her self discipline to keep her hands off him in the car.

It was a gloriously sunny afternoon, made even more special by the joyous possibility that maybe summer wasn't quite done for the year yet. The garden looked like a scene from a fairy tale. Even the trees sparkled with diamante decorations. Well, Tabitha assumed that they weren't real diamonds but who knew. The Brinkleys were reportedly extremely rich and an invite to their annual shindig was coveted by many. Gary's firm had been providing investment advice to the family for many generations so were on the invite list every year.

It was a chance for all of the guests to celebrate, both their business and personal achievements together, hobnob a little and also an opportunity for some very rich people to provide donations for good causes.

Later there would be an auction, providing funds for the children's ward at the local hospital. Last year Tabitha had sat, gobsmacked at the mind-blowing amounts being pledged and had made very sure not to let her hand twitch in error while the bidding was taking place.

As they crossed the lawn, greeted by enthusiastic offers of an array of welcome drinks and canapes, Gary's boss, Lionel Wilkes waved over to them. Tabitha adored him and his wife, Sandra. She had met them for the first time when Mrs Wilkes had taken Tabitha under her more experienced wing very quickly last year, sensing her newbie nerves. Handshakes and hugs were exchanged all round.

"It's lovely to see you dear", exclaimed Mrs Wilkes. "You kids look to die for. Oh Lionel darling, do you remember when we were young?"

Mr Wilkes bent his back over and raised a curved hand to his ear. "Sorry dear. Did you say something? I don't have my ear horn with me."

The group laughed together and Mr Wilkes continued cheerfully. "We're not for seed just yet dear. You are still stopping young men in their tracks. Oh Tabitha, Gary, you really must check out the cakes when you get a chance. My Sandra grilled the coffee and walnut and rather splendid it is too."

"Ah thank you dear", chuckled Sandra. "I actually baked it." She winked at Tabitha and Gary. "There is a marvellous spread over there. I literally had to wrestle Lionel away from the Shrimp. I'm pretty sure there is a limit on how much of it you should consume in one go!"

Tabitha glanced over at the long trestle tables, adorned with delicious looking food. Note to self, she thought. Do not spill cocktail sauce down your dress. You will not look, or in fact, smell good. Maybe she wouldn't even attempt to eat Shrimp in front of all of these people. Even bitesize food seemed to succeed in ending up on her chin instead of in her mouth in these types of situations.

Last year she had been too nervous to even risk it being a dilemma and after a whole afternoon of abstaining from eating, she had persuaded Gary to stop at a fast food drive thru on the way home, much to his light hearted but still evident disdain.

As Tabitha contemplated how on earth she was going to get through this entire event without doing something embarrassing, a stunningly put together goddess seemed to literally float over to their group.

"Oh Vanessa darling, there you are." Mr Wilkes popped a hand affectionately on the goddess's back, a goddess who now had a name, surprisingly just a human name. "I was hoping to introduce you to Tabitha. Finally there are more people here your age sweetheart. Tabitha is Gary's delightful girlfriend. Tabitha, this is our daughter, Vanessa."

" It's lovely to meet you Vanessa." Tabitha smiled warmly and held out her hand.

Vanessa was dressed in a fitted, pin striped trouser suit. Her short blonde hair was slicked back glamorously. Tabitha concluded admiringly that she was only a monocle and a pink bodice away from being Madonna in her Express yourself video.

A well-manicured hand with blood red nail varnish reached out and accepted Tabitha's handshake. "Ah, so you're Tabitha. I've heard lots about you."

Mr Wilkes looked on fondly at the young people making each other's acquaintance. "So, Vanessa finally came to work for the company a few months ago. I've been shamelessly headhunting my own daughter since she finished studying design and management at university and now I've finally managed to entice her to join us."

He gestured delightedly at Vanessa and Scott. "These two are becoming quite the dynamic duo Tabitha."

Tabitha could see the pride that this dear man clearly had for his daughter. "Ah that's lovely Mr Wilkes. It's really great to meet you Vanessa."

It was nice that Vanessa had heard about her. She didn't really have Gary down for the type of guy who would talk about her with his colleagues to be honest but she was delighted to be proved wrong.

Vanessa smiled widely at each of them in turn. "Anyway. I'll be back. I must circulate a little. After all, we are surrounded by lots of rich people who are full of champagne and bravado." She rubbed her hands together gleefully.

Tabitha wasn't quite sure whether she was joking or not, especially as she continued on. "Perfect pickings for new clients. Anybody is up for grabs if you want them enough."

Tabitha felt certain that Vanessa's wink was mostly directed at Gary as she said this and guessed that it must be an inside joke from the office. Vanessa went and sidled up to a nearby group, surreptitiously listening in to their conversation, laughing at the correct time, then apologising for intruding and introducing herself. Wow, she was good.

Gary politely excused Tabitha and himself from the Wilkes' and they wandered over to check out the auction prizes. A weekend in Paris, A Helicopter ride over London, Season tickets for Arsenal. Good gracious, Tabitha was chuffed if she could afford to travel to three Reading away games in a season.

"Hey lovebirds, how are you doing?" They both jumped at the loud voice behind them.

"Hey Steve", they chorused. Steve planted a kiss on Tabitha's cheek then looked around animatedly.

"I've just got to pop to the loo but then I need to hang with you gorgeous people, ok. Back in a min", and he was gone again.

Steve tended to pop to the loo quite frequently, due to the unfortunate powder addiction that he had acquired whilst working ridiculous hours in the city. Tabitha wasn't quite sure how he got away with his drug taking with Mr Wilkes as he wasn't exactly very discreet. It was such a shame that he felt the need to use, even on a day like today. He was a really great guy and Tabitha suspected that he didn't really need any assistance in being the life and soul of any gathering.

Tabitha accepted another glass of Pimms from a young lad who actually kind of bowed to her. She kind of bowed back as she thanked him and she and Gary found a table that they could watch the festivities from. There was a maypole set up for the children and Tabitha laughed and flinched in equal measures as the excited little dancers got themselves into quite a tangle.

She spotted Mr and Mrs Brinkley working their way around the gardens. They looked like royalty and, in the same manner as the queen, appeared to have a conversation prepared for each of their many guests. It was quite impressive to watch.

The sun shone down brightly on the merry gathering and Tabitha felt a warm joy at being a part of it, no longer a novice, proudly sitting beside her man.

Steve came lolloping back across the grass with three shot glasses in his hand.

"Tequila, my friends? Oh, or are you driving Gary? Shame, that'll be two for you then Tabitha. Makes up for you missing Brighton. I hope you're feeling better now…oh unless you have something to share with us and can't drink at all?" He looked at her tummy inquisitively.

Tabitha saw Gary's jaw tense up as confusion whirled around in her head. What was Steve talking about? Missing Brighton? Why would Gary have said that she was ill and why had he not invited her to Brighton if she had been welcome? She had just assumed that it was a boy's trip of some sort.

She felt hurt but mostly annoyed that she had now immediately lost her relaxed feeling of fitting in and belonging here amongst these people. Well, this was certainly not the time or place to address it. It would have to keep for now. After all, there must be a rational explanation. Gary would explain everything later, she was sure. Nevertheless, she was cross that she now felt unsettled.

She dug deep to summon her best smile. "I'm quite fine, thanks Steve. Tequila seems like a marvellous idea, thank you." She picked up a glass, willing her hand to be steadier than it felt and raised it to clink Steve's glass. "Bottoms up ay?"

"Maybe be a little careful hon. You haven't eaten mu."

A darted look from Tabitha stopped Gary in his tracks.

Tabitha responded decisively. "As I said dear. I'm quite well. Please don't fret."

Steve laughed at their little exchange, unaware that there was anything behind what he thought was just couple's banter. He knocked back a tequila and jumped up, clapping his hands together to draw their attention back to him. "Dance with me Tabitha, perlease. They are teaching the Gay Gordons over there and I haven't got a girl. Can I steal her away Gary?"

"Sure, of course", smiled Gary. "Take care of her though buddy. I know you have two left feet."

Steve held out his hand and led Tabitha across the grass. A group of enthusiastic guests were trying in earnest to follow the instructions that were being shouted frantically over the noise of the bagpiper. The majority of the revellers were tripping over each other and laughing hysterically. One couple who seemed to know what they were doing were trying unsuccessfully to steer people in something resembling the right direction.

"I'm not sure I have the right shoes on for this but hey ho, what's the worst that can happen?" giggled Tabitha.

"I wouldn't worry gal. This looks more like the Stray Gordons than the Gay Gordons!"

Steve placed Tabitha at the end of the line of ladies and stepped back into his own position. Before they knew it, and due to the other participants being so awful, they found that they were only second best to the couple who looked like they partook in Scottish country dancing every weekend.

Tabitha squinted over to see if Gary was watching their triumph but he was engrossed in conversation. She saw his head fall back in hysterical laughter as he reached out his hand and placed it on Vanessa's arm.

Tabitha wasn't ordinarily a jealous person but the scene made her tummy jolt. Steve followed her gaze.

"Oh Tabby. I am simply so in love with that woman. Isn't she divine?"

"Yes, quite beautiful", Tabitha agreed, trying to refocus on the task at hand and work out which foot she should now be putting forward.

"I think she knows though. Not that she's beautiful I don't mean", Steve quickly clarified, "but that I am besottedly infatuated with her. That's why she keeps safer company and chooses to hang out with your Gary. You should have seen them do karaoke last weekend. I was well jealous. 'Islands in the stream…'", he sang dreamily and twirled around, bumping clumsily into the man next to him.

"Oops sorry. My bad mate. I'm so so sorry", he chuckled.

"Maybe we should quit while we're ahead Steve." Tabitha gently steered him away from danger. "I don't know about you but I could maybe do with eating something?"

They headed back to their table with a couple of plates of food to share.

"That was great guys." Gary moved along a seat so that they could sit back down, putting himself irritatingly, even closer to Vanessa.

Tabitha felt herself stew inside. He hadn't even been looking at their dancing. There was no need to humour them. They weren't six, for heaven's sake. And since when would he willingly participate in karaoke? It was the type of thing that he would usually dismiss as juvenile.

"Can I get you a drink Vanessa?" Steve offered, his pupils even more dilated now that he was looking at her, than they had been previously just from his illegal stimulants.

"Thanks Stevie, you're a doll but I need to make a move shortly. I have a private pilates sesh booked at mine. These love handles aren't gonna banish themselves. You know how it is, Tabitha," she added, unnecessarily and rather rudely, Tabitha felt..

Tabitha rolled her eyes as both of the boys looked, as was her obvious intention, at Vanessa's slim waist and firm behind with no sign of any room for love handles.

"Ah that's a shame Vanessa. It was lovely to meet you though. Cheerio." Tabitha did her best to look sorry that she was leaving. Then she knocked back the extra Tequila shot with as much aggression as she could muster, forcing herself not to pull the expression that she wanted to, as even the smell made her feel a little queasy now.

If this girl wanted to do battle, Tabitha was going to show her that she was no pushover and that she could handle both herself and her liquor. The lump in her throat stopped the Tequila from going down smoothly though and she let out a loud uncouth hiccup.

"Oh dear, water for you next maybe, sweet pea", Vanessa laughed patronisingly. "See y'all later. I must say toodles to Ma and Pa."

She glided away, which Tabitha noted should not have been possible in heels that high and pointy. Her perfume continued to linger in the air, long after she was out of sight.

Steve screwed his face into a disappointed pout. "Oh bugger. That's a mighty damn shame. Right, I'm gonna check out the stalls guys. It's Mum's birthday next week. There must be necklaces and homemade jam around here somewhere." He sped off towards the row of white pagodas on his next quest.

Tabitha turned to face Gary, realising that she now found herself in unfamiliar territory.

"What's going on hon? Why didn't you want to invite me to Brighton and why would you lie about me being ill?"

Gary somehow had the audacity to look shocked that the matter was being raised then he shifted uncomfortably in his seat, looking like a kid who had been caught stealing conkers.

"It was all just gonna be too worky", he offered. "I thought you'd get bored."

"Oh, and yet today, I'm welcome?" As your accessory!, Tabitha added silently in her head. "It wasn't all work though was it?", she continued. "Karaoke for example. What's really going on here?" she asked whilst holding her false smile for any onlookers.

Gary put a hand on Tabitha's knee. "It's nothing much really."

"Nothing much. What the hell does that mean?"

Gary looked around them frantically as if he was seeking any kind of escape just as Mr and Mrs Brinkley walked over to them.

"Miss Morris, Mr Saunders, how lovely to see you both", exclaimed Mr Brinkley as they approached.

Gary sprung up from his seat and shook their hands with cringe-inducing enthusiasm. Tabitha got to her feet slowly, trying to steady herself as she did so, the alcohol and uncertainty appearing to be quite an intoxicating combination. Her movement was still too quick though and the gardens swam blurrily around her, forcing her to sit back down.

"Oh dear. Are you feeling ok sweetheart?", enquired Mrs Brinkley. "This built up heat can do terrible things for one's balance", she said as she glanced down at the empty shot glasses on the table.

"Goodness, I do beg your pardon please." Tabitha took a deep breath. "I seem to have been developing a migraine as the afternoon has gone on. I had so much fun dancing too but I fear that we may need to miss the auction."

"Oh my dear girl." Mrs Brinkley smiled reassuringly at them both. "Don't you worry. I used to suffer with terrible migraines myself until I found this wonderful acupuncturist. I'll send his details to you through Mr Wilkes."

"That is so kind of you Mrs Brinkley, thank you. Oh, and Gary was hoping to leave a sizeable donation with you as we won't be here for the auction, weren't you darling?"

CHAPTER SIX

Tabitha remained silent on the drive home. Random words from the afternoon tumbled messily around in her head and it felt as though they were bumping on the edges of her temples as they went. The conversation that needed to be had was not appropriate whilst Gary was driving and, to be frank, she had no idea where she was even going to begin.

Eventually they pulled into her driveway and Gary turned off the engine. "Um. Should I come in?" he ventured, looking rather pale himself now.

"I don't actually know Gary", Tabitha sighed, " I mean, what did you mean by 'It's nothing much really'?"

Gary fidgeted with the St Christopher pendant on his dashboard, evidently looking for any guidance or even divine intervention to get out of the predicament he had found himself in.

"Well Tabs, if you really want me to be honest..."

"Of course I want you to be bloody honest, you idiot", she cried, although doubting if she really meant it.

"Ok. So there is an attraction between Vanessa and me".

Tabitha felt her whole body shudder. Her eyes began to blur but there was no way that she was going to allow herself to cry in front of him. 'Vanessa and I', she corrected in her head and then questioned herself, then wondered why the flippin' hell punctuation was important right now.

"And....well.. there was....a kiss. But we were playing Truth or dare."

"What the actual fff? Gary, are you crazy? How could you? How long have you known that you liked her?"

"Um?"

"Honestly Gary."

"A few months I guess". He hung his head. "But it was just an attraction. Not like how I feel about you. And we had such a lovely holiday and I do think that we have a strong future together."

"So the kiss was before the holiday?"

"Um....No. It was Saturday night in Brighton."

Tabitha felt sick with the reality of how this was all unfolding. Now feeling remarkably sober, the start of a hangover wasn't helping her either. How was she supposed to keep her cool when she had been so blindsided and made to feel so stupid?

Now, on reflection, she realised that he had been more and more distant, even before the holiday and certainly after. Was this why he had kept trying to spend money on her, especially in Greece. Guilt money? For some reason 'Blood money' by Jon Bon Jovi started playing in her head. What the..? She suddenly felt like such a fool for thinking that he had been busy at work, toiling for their future, when he had just been distracted by perfect bloody Vanessa. Another thought suddenly filled her with horror.

"So it was a work trip! Who else was playing Truth or dare with you Gary? Who else there today was aware of what a prat you've made of me?" She rubbed her temples vigorously. "Truth or dare for God's sake Gary. We're twenty five, not fifteen."

Gary sat tight lipped. She looked at his beautiful jawline, tense from the confrontation, a repeated nervous twitch now dwelled in the dimple that she loved so much and she was broken hearted at how she couldn't make this all better for him. She couldn't hold him and make his problems go away.

"Who else was playing Gary?" she asked despairingly.

"Nobody else….It was just the two of us."

With that, Tabitha grabbed her bag and opened the car door. It took all of her strength to pull herself upright out of the seat..

"You can go to hell Gary Saunders", she screamed, slamming the door hard behind her. "How bloody dare you."

She held her head high as she marched indoors, before collapsing into hiccupping sobs on the carpet as soon as she was safely out of his sight.

CHAPTER SEVEN

As Tabitha awoke the following morning, she willed for yesterday to have just been a bad dream. If she stayed safely tucked underneath the duvet with her eyes shut tight, then maybe it would all go away and her perfect life would be back again.

But sadly this wasn't to be the case. As the name Vanessa Wilkes began to echo around in her throbbing head, she gradually had to face up to the horrid realisation that it had been real life and also that, shamefully, she had slept in her beautiful red dress because of that silly silly man.

How could he be so duplicitous? It had been his idea to go on holiday together, leading to her thinking, all the more, that they'd had a future together. And that decision had been made by him after he had met the incredible Vanessa. Tabitha felt like she just didn't know him at all now.

After a shower, she paced anxiously from room to room, feeling like the walls were swaying eerily and closing in on her. She had to get out. She needed to run. She pulled on her trainers and headed towards the sports centre in the park. She was relieved to find the sprinting track clear of any other runners this morning. She certainly had no desire to exchange pleasantries with anybody right now. She just needed to find some exertion therapy and quickly. She charged around the track, pounding the floor, almost trying to kick out the memory of yesterday's conversation with each step.

When she could run no more, she staggered to lean on a nearby tree, trying to catch her breath. She fought off the sickness that now rose in her throat from both the mental and physical exhaustion she was experiencing. She needed a plan. Even just a little one. A one hour at a time plan.

She slumped down on to the dewy grass and looked up searchingly at the moody sky. As the clouds expanded to darken her view she felt so incredibly small in the scheme of everything, like a nervous ant, fearing the potential of being trodden on and thereby snuffed out at any moment.

As she gazed mournfully at the high tangled tree branches above her, two beautiful white butterflies suddenly came into her view and danced together nearby. As she watched them, daringly flitting closer and closer to her, she felt a welcomed warmth, like they had maybe put a soothing spell on her. Much needed energy began to spread slowly through her weary body and she pulled herself slowly back up to her feet.

Ok, plan one. Go home and feed Snuggles. Her poor fur baby wasn't to know all that had happened with Gary and would be frankly quite dismayed at his mistress' negligence. After all, Tabitha had only just been forgiven for the audacity of leaving him to the kindness of others for ten days while she was on holiday.

That was a start, Tabitha thought as she headed towards the park gate and rustled in her hoodie pocket for her keys. As she pulled out nothing but a used tissue and a Lidl receipt, she pictured her keys lying on the hallway carpet where she had dropped them along with her handbag yesterday. Darn. Now what?

She quickly established that she wasn't ready to see her Mother just yet. She would only crumble if she was anywhere near a hug from her Mum right now and she really needed to try to be tough, at least until she decided what to do next.

She remembered that, thankfully, Pam still had a spare key for her place after being one of Snuggles' kind visitors. Tabitha wondered if she would actually be up this early on a Sunday though. She did a 180 and headed off in her direction, realising that she might have to open up, at least a little, about what had happened yesterday to explain her early intrusion. She wondered if Pam would even be shocked. She hadn't always appeared to be Gary's biggest fan in the first place but this? Seriously?

Tabitha thought about the amount of times that she had defended him to her friends and had made excuses for his, now even more infuriating, dismissiveness towards them and their activities. She should have taken notice of those people that cared about her. She shouldn't have been so damn submissive to the wants and goals in his life above her own.

Her eyes filled with hot tears again. However, she was glad to realise that now some of her tears were already fuelled by anger and not just sadness.

Cool rain began to drizzle down on her as she walked along. It felt good after her run and she held her face up to the sky, welcoming the refreshing drops. She savoured the rustling sound as she gently kicked through the dry leaves that were beginning to fall with the approach of Autumn. The noise reminded her of being young and carefree and gave her a much needed comfort.

By the time she turned into Pam's road, her hair was coated to the sides of her face and she found it strangely amusing as a raindrop plopped from the end of her nose to the ground. What a sight she would be for poor Pam.

Suddenly she jumped as a loud beep made her aware that there were, in fact, other people existing right now despite her inward blurred thoughts. She looked up to see her brother, George waving cheerily from his van. She waved back, surprised to see him out and about this way. As he passed by her, he squirted his windscreen spray and swished his wipers, visibly giggling as it added to her water issues. She found herself laughing though which felt quite splendid. Only George would get away with that behaviour right now.

Throughout their lives, he'd always had a cheeky prank up his sleeve to cheer up her mood, even when he didn't realise it was required. What great timing that she had seen him. She knew that laughter breeds more happiness in oneself when feeling down but found that the theory wasn't always easy to put into practice.

Feeling slightly better now, and like she may just survive the day, well the hour at least, she headed up to Pam's door and rang the bell, praying that her pal would forgive her if she was rudely waking her up.

"Just coming", shouted Pam as she flung the door wide open and laughed, "What did you forget Geor…."

Pam's mouth fell open as she saw Tabitha standing on the doorstep. "Oh it's you", she exclaimed, wide eyed, peering around her to look along the road.

"Oh that's nice hon. Who were you expecting?...Oh!!" Tabitha's mouth now also fell open as the penny dropped as she realised what Pam had just said as she'd opened the door. Pam simultaneously screwed up her face and held her hand to her mouth.

"Oh!" exclaimed Tabitha again, taking in Pam's dressing gown.

"Oh!" agreed Pam. "You'd better come in hon. I guess it's time for us to have a chat."

Pam ushered Tabitha through to the kitchen and quickly cleared the empty bottle and two wine glasses away from the night before.

"Um, sit down hon. You're drenched. Do you want a coffee?" Pam looked slightly terrified.

"Sure, thanks", agreed Tabitha, hunting to find words that she could string together to let her friend know that she wasn't upset about George, although mightily shocked at whatever was going on. She had to somehow explain to her friend though that she was, in fact, reeling from the disaster of her own love life.

She watched her dear friend, Pam as she purposefully spooned coffee into the mugs, seemingly taking her time whilst also thinking of what to say. It wasn't like either of them to ever be short of words, especially with each other, but this was, well, this was an unexpected turn of events to say the least. Her dear friend and her dear brother being together. If they were in fact together? Were they actually together together?

Well, whatever they were, it was lovely, she decided. It was just like something out of one of her favourite sitcoms.

It was everything else that was pants though. The overwhelming emotions of yesterday suddenly came back over her again like a huge wave, now that she was here in a safe place.

Pam felt her breath catch in her throat as she readied herself to explain to Tabitha about her and George having unexpectedly become closer over a period of time. She was sure that it would be ok once she came clean and explained that her intentions with her brother were honourable. Tabitha was a reasonable person and they had been friends forever. Yeah it would be fine she thought until she turned round with their coffees to find Tabitha with her head in her hands, sobbing her heart out.

CHAPTER EIGHT

Once Pamela was up to speed with yesterday's awful revelations, she wished that Tabitha had just been upset about discovering her and George's secret romance.

She especially couldn't get her head around him having the audacity to take Tabitha along to the function when he'd known full well that his side piece was going to be there. She tried to articulate her thoughts and get it all clear in her head. "So he…? But he….?" Nope, there was actually nothing.

How could this have happened to her beautiful friend? Tabitha was the kindest soul that she had ever met. Pretty, smart and funny. In her opinion she had always been far too obliging to Gary's every self absorbed whim. Oh, how she wished that she could give him even a small piece of her mind right now.

She held her friend's trembling hand. "Hon, you know what. If he is that bloody fickle then at least you have found out now. You could have been married to that shit with a couple of kiddies in tow one day, hosting his soirees, or whatever you call them, for his…" She paused to try to think of a suitable client type word but the mist clouded the part of her brain used for communicating…. "his…." She banged her fist on the table angrily, "Smarmy people!" She finished her sentence unsatisfactorily but quite decisively nevertheless.

Tabitha jumped as the coffee cups rattled precariously on the table. She was dismayed that a situation that she was part of, had made her friend this upset but she also realised that she found it weirdly amusing to witness her being so punchy. Pam was usually pretty chilled and seeing her having an absolute bee in her bonnet reminded Tabitha of when a school teacher would get wound up and you would have to try not to laugh, at the risk of receiving a detention. Before she could help it, Tabitha had let out a small snort.

Pam stared at her, startled. "What is? What are? Sorry, just WHAT?"

Tabitha shook her head, unable to explain, as Pam's face, now baffled as well as still pretty miffed, just really tickled her. She tried so hard to keep it together but before she knew it, a new batch of tears were pouring down her cheeks. Tears of absolute mirth.

"Oh glory be", Tabitha panted. "I don't know wha….." The more she tried to speak, the worse it got so she decided to just concentrate on breathing for the time being.

She could only assume that this latest episode was due to the build-up of emotions that she had forced herself to hold in whilst in public yesterday afternoon. She had been so proud of herself that she had managed not to cry until she had been safely at home alone, but now apparently, a further release of some form of delirium was on the cards and she just couldn't pull herself together.

Poor Pam looked completely bewildered as Tabitha held her aching tummy and waved her other hand around, indicating that she would, almost certainly, be fine in just a moment.

After a few minutes she finally managed to bring herself back under control. As both girls wondered if Tabitha may have just had some kind of emotional breakdown, they fell silent apart from Tabitha's deep, calm-restoring breaths. The kitchen clock ticked loudly, bringing them back to the reality of here and now.

"So, anyways", Tabitha concluded, sucking in her cheeks to form a resigned pout. "It is what it is. Oh, but Pammy, I'm so pleased that I came here. I only came to get a key for my place."

Pam squeezed her friend's shoulder affectionately.

"I'm so pleased that you came here too. We're gonna get you through this my lovely. You do know that don't you? You don't need a man to make your life great, especially a buffoon like that."

Tabitha momentarily felt the customary urge to defend Gary, at least a little, then realised she had no idea why. No more. This was it.

Although she still couldn't quite believe that it had all fallen apart so quickly. But then, she concluded, it hadn't been as quick as she thought. It had been unravelling for a while, it seemed. She just hadn't been a party to that information.

She fought to clear the whirlwind of internal discussion in her own head and smiled at her friend.

"Anyway, talking of buffoons. Do you have anything you'd like to share now about my brother? Not too much though obvs." Tabitha screwed up her face in preparation as she asked, realising that there were now probably some girlie conversations that Pam would simply need to have with other friends.

The look in Pam's eyes as she talked about her and George's blossoming 'relationship' was totally heart-warming. Tabitha wondered how she hadn't noticed that they had been catching 'the feels' for each other. Maybe she just didn't notice anything anymore when it came to matters of the heart.

Tabitha had always felt protective over George when it came to women, regardless of him being her older sibling. Despite his cheekiness, he had a heart of gold and there was no way some girl was gonna take advantage of him but this was all sounding really rather exciting. She knew that whatever transpired between Pam and George, they would treat each other with respect and they could be really good for each other.

Even without knowingly spending time with them yet as a couple, listening to Pam now, Tabitha could already recognise elements that they seemed to possess which had been lacking from her relationship with Gary.

Getting over Gary Saunders might not be quick but she darn well would be ok.

CHAPTER NINE

As Tabitha walked into the office the next morning, she could sense an excited energy, which was uncommon indeed for a dull and drizzly Monday. Work, it transpired, was about to become a joyful distraction from her dismantled love life.

Tabitha felt as though there were a lot of eyes on her as she headed for her desk and she quickly checked that she wasn't still wearing her slippers or trailing toilet paper on her shoe.

"What's going on hon?", she whispered to her desk buddy, Marnie who was usually in the know.

"Read your email babe. You're a Goddamn superstar, that's what."

Tabitha sat down, feeling a little befuddled and waited for what seemed like forever for her computer to load up.

She scanned down the list of new emails quickly. There were twelve new messages with three of them looking strangely like they had been sent directly to her from the 'big bosses' whose names she only recognised from their bi-annual company conventions.

She opened a message from her line manager first, hoping that this would bring some clarity to the situation. The bold letters sprung from the page.

Huge congratulations to our own Tabitha Morris for being offered the opportunity to work with Yerans on their new advertising campaign.

Oh goodness. Oh, that'll be it then. Tabitha's hand flew to her mouth in astonishment as she also realised just how many people were copied in to the announcement. She glanced quickly around the office at her beaming colleagues before reading on.

We competed against the biggest and best advertising companies for this project and our Tabitha has secured the contract, based on her portfolio and initial ideas. A shining example to us all that we can achieve anything, even if we are a smaller company, so long as we believe in our ability and concepts. Have a great week everybody!

Tabitha looked up at a very excited Marnie as her colleagues, Peter and Kelly bundled over eagerly.

"This is massive, Tabitha. These adverts will be seen round half the world, you do realise that?", enthused Peter.

"No pressure hon", laughed Kelly, patting her on the back as Tabitha shook her head, trying to find a space for this to sink in.

Yerans were a huge brand. She had even seen their food products in Greece, and at a premium at that, as they were so sought after by holidaymakers looking for a little bit of home comfort. She guessed they were akin to her Mum always taking a pot of marmite on holiday, 'just in case' although she even did that when they went to Cornwall 'just in case'!

Tabitha had been close to pointing the products out to Gary when she'd spotted them in a shop near their hotel. She'd wanted to tell him about her proposal to work with them but she hadn't thought for a moment that she would actually get the contract and she didn't want to bore him with something that might not even be a thing.

Lizzie, her line manager came over and joined the happy group. "Ok peeps. I know this is awesome and I'm sorry to put the celebrations on hold, but Tabitha, I will be stealing you away in half an hour. We need to go through some of the finer details so have a coffee and enjoy these people's faces while you can cos you're gonna be a very busy girl".

Lizzie almost sang the end of her sentence and Peter clapped his hands together excitedly like a seal. The girls all looked at him in astonishment.

"Sorry, too much guys?", he laughed. "I just knew you had it in you Tabby." The others nodded in agreement.

Half an hour, one coffee and two nervous wees later, Tabitha sat in a meeting room with Lizzie.

"So, first things first", Lizzie began. "Yes, this is awesome. Yes, this is amazing but more importantly, it's actually not."

Tabitha peered over her glasses, feeling confused. Not a great start, she mused to herself.

Lizzie continued. "It's not awesome and amazing because it is totally deserved. You are a great ideas person and that's why they want you, why they chose you. Honey, that's why they need you. Yerans loved your ideas for increasing the brand's appeal to the food on the move market. Everybody is running around all over the place. Their brand is in 60% of households in over 27 countries but they still have to move with the times and it's you that's gonna be moving them. Your proposed timing of the adverts also fits in with the launch of their new environmentally friendly packaging so it'll be a double whammy....I think the word whammy can be used for a good thing."

Tabitha nodded and shrugged at the same time, not completely sure herself. She took a breath to speak but Lizzie was far too enthused to take a break. She waved her hands around dramatically as she continued on.

"Darling, we're talking TV adverts, Radio adverts, Billboards, the whole shebang. They are prepared to spend a lot so if you want celebs, you'll get celebs. Whatever you want, you just let them know."

"Uh huh." Tabitha agreed, scribbling on her notepad.

Lizzie smiled and pointed her pen at Tabitha. "Any questions from you at the moment?"

Tabitha laughed. "I think you've covered everything for now. I'll get straight on it."

"Fab. Thatagirl. I'm not going to interfere at all unless you need me but I'm here and even if I'm not here, I am. We'll set up an initial meeting for you with their team on...um...Friday morning?"

"That sounds perfect Lizzie. Thank you."

Tabitha was pleased that she sounded more confident about what was ahead of her than she actually felt right now and assessed that that could be a helpful asset in the coming weeks.

"Splendid. One last thing. My boss has given me a credit note from his boss for the team to have drinks to celebrate." Lizzie looked like she herself might burst from the recognition received for her staff member. "Does Friday evening, straight from work, sound good?"

"That'll be amazing. Thanks. I'll let people know."

Lizzie held her hand up abruptly. "No darling, I'll let people know. I don't want you to be concerned with anything except for getting your ideas down. You need anything else cleared or done, you just let me know."

Tabitha beamed. "Thanks so much Lizzie. This is exciting".

As they left the meeting room Lizzie took her arm. "Just remember Tabitha, you deserve this."

As soon as Tabitha got in the door that evening she dialled her Mum's number.

"Tabitha darling, I was hoping you'd call."

"Hi Mum", panted Tabitha. "I have news."

"Oh my darling, I know. Your brother told me. What a pig."

"Who's a Pig? George?"

"No love, Gary. Ooh your brother was fuming. It was all I could do to stop him from calling him. He said he'd never liked him in the first place cos he always thought he was better than everyone else. Then I said, 'well if you never liked him, then it's good you don't have to spend a lifetime of Christmases with him after all isn't it.'"

Tabitha's Mum paused briefly as if looking for at least some indication of agreement or even approval before she continued on.

"Anyway love, he seemed to calm down a bit then but that Pig wants to stay out of his way for a bit or he'll get a good telling off and quite right too."

Tabitha couldn't help but smile. What was it with not being able to get a word in edgeways today.

"Are you still there love? Are you ok?"

"Yes Mum, I'm here", Tabitha laughed. "I actually called about other news though."

By the end of the call, Tabitha's Mother was all of a fluster again but now in a good way.

"I'm so proud of you sweetheart. Well I had written you a poem to help you get over that fool but it seems like you've got this yourself. That's my fabby Tabby. I'll text it to you anyway. It needs a little tweaking but I'm quite proud of it, but not as proud as I am of you, my munchkin."

"Thanks Mum. Well if I'm a munchkin, you're definitely the good witch Glinda."

Tabitha's phone pinged just after they signed off and she read her Mum's poem.

When it seems that all is lost my dear
don't let it make you fall
cos 'all' may not have been the thing
that made you stand up tall

It may feel it was the biggest piece
but you lived your life before
and even if this piece is gone
you still have so much more
So smile brave one, you'll see a day
when this was just the reason
to gather yourself together again
and find a richer season

Tabitha was reminded, once again, where she had got her flair for words from, which had ended up giving her the career that she loved. She messaged straight back.

I love it Mum. You really should share your work Xx

Ah thanks sweetie. I'll send you my fave poem that I wrote the other day later. Best title ever - Hidden peas! Xx

Tabitha laid in bed that night with the day's crazy events whizzing around in her head excitedly. Mum's hidden peas poem had been really catchy. It was sharp and it stuck, even after just a couple of reads. Good rhymes could do that. Mmm Yes, that could work...rhymes....Radio jingles....TV ads....Her mind started working overtime now.

So we are going for food on the move. So where would people like to eat their Yerans products?

I like my Yerans at my nan's - Ok, interesting start. Who is famous for loving their nan? Or maybe the famous person could be the nan? The Queen maybe? Now don't be silly, she thought. Even Yerans couldn't get the real Queen.

We like our Yerans in our vans – Builders, Delivery drivers, Ooh ice cream vans?

We like our Yerans with the fans - Football or Rugby players starring?

We like our Yerans whilst getting spray tans - reality star needed or possibly the Football or Rugby player again, she laughed to herself.

We like our Yerans round at Dan's - Dan Carter and the New Zealand rugby team? Daniel Radcliffe and the cast of Harry Potter? Sure, because none of them would be busy with other engagements.

Tabitha decided that her imagination was starting to run a little bit too wild now but at least she had some ideas. She went to sleep with a very cheery outlook.

CHAPTER TEN

Tabitha's positive outlook was proved well founded at her meeting the following Friday. It was a huge success and really enjoyable. The team at Yerans that she would be working with had been really enthusiastic as she'd shared her ideas. They were so fun and welcoming that she felt guilty that she'd been nervous about meeting them. Of course, they were in marketing so they were all on pretty much the same page. With their parting sentiments being that they were certain that the campaign would be a fantastic triumph, Tabitha finally began to believe what Lizzy had said and realise her own worth.

As she and her colleagues poured into the bar that evening, Tabitha felt an overwhelming feeling of happiness and wellbeing. She also realised that she had regained a sense of freedom that she hadn't really noticed that she'd lost. She hadn't had to consider whether her plans this evening would fit in with Gary's, her former priority. Now her time was primarily hers which, looking back now, hadn't actually been the case for a while. That wasn't necessarily all Gary's fault but he hadn't done anything to stop it either. Well, until now!

Tabitha felt herself blush as Kelly led a toast to her success but she accepted her colleagues' congratulations gratefully. She was absolutely buzzing from her day and she finally silently agreed that she did deserve this and allowed herself to soak up the approval of her team. No longer would she be a backbencher, clapping loudly and supportively for Gary's successes. Now it was time to allow herself to shine in her own life.

Tabitha was soon brought back to earth a little though when they all went through to the games room to play darts. Peter made his despair known to the group immediately when he was paired up with her and his fears weren't unfounded. Tabitha concluded that maybe she should stick to being in charge of the scoring like she usually did when her friend's played.

The team supped through their freebie drinks at an impressive speed and, with passionate declarations that they should all do this more often, the gathering eventually dwindled down to Tabitha, Kelly, Marnie and Peter.

They headed back into the main bar to discover that it was now heaving, full of people diving headfirst into the weekend. A stage had been set up all ready for an open mic night.

"Oh wow", squealed Marnie. "Guys we absolutely have to do a song."

"Don't we need to be able to play an instrument or be..um...talented?", enquired Tabitha, hoping desperately that there were rules against them joining in and making fools of themselves.

"Nah, it's just for fun", Kelly argued. "They'll let us sing, I'm sure. I'm gonna ask them to write our names down." Kelly was gone before Tabitha could stop her.

"I'm with you", Peter grumbled, looking horrified. "I have no desire to get up there and make a prat of myself. I'm heading out for a smoke while these crazy buggers seal the fate of our reputations in this town."

Tabitha laughed. "I'll come out with you. I could do with some fresh air. Maybe we can just leg it without them seeing."

They headed out the front doors to the smoking area where a group of shivering bodies huddled closely together by the solitary heater. Peter lit up a cigarette and pulled an unimpressed face as he inhaled deeply. "Tastes like shit", he huffed as he took another drag.

Tabitha was confused. "If you don't like it, why on earth are you doing it?"

Peter shrugged. "Dunno really. My missus keeps asking me the same question. She hates me smoking. I'm just addicted I guess but I'm well over it. Smoking is defo overrated"

Tabitha didn't want to point out to her friend that she wasn't sure that cigarettes had actually been rated as a good thing at all since about the 1930s when they were advertised as a cure for sore throats before their negative effects had been discovered. She had thankfully never tried to smoke so hadn't personally had to face the tough battle of quitting.

Peter took another few drags in quick succession, looking like he was trying to get the experience over with.

"My filthy mistress, be away with your tarry seduction", he exclaimed and stepped on the cigarette halfway through.

Tabitha smiled at him, thinking that maybe he could try comedy for his open mic moment. "Ya know, my brother has been vaping for a while hon. It's not ideal if you ask me but it's definitely a step in the right direction. Maybe give it a go."

"Mmm", said Peter, not looking convinced. "One day maybe. Right, let's see what hell awaits us back in there."

"You know what", laughed Tabitha. "What's the worst that can happen?"

They paused and looked at each other, united in fear, as everything that was the worst that could happen flashed before their eyes.

As they headed reluctantly back towards the door, Tabitha was halted by the sound of a familiar laugh. She turned to see Scott walking past with a couple of friends.

"Hey Scott", she hollered, realising at the sound that maybe the shot of Sambuca she'd had earlier had hit the spot harder than she'd thought it had.

Scott looked round and headed over, smiling broadly. "Hi Tabby, what are you doing this end of town?"

He looked inquisitively at Peter who in turn protectively linked his arm through Tabitha's.

"Ah we all came out straight from work and thought this was the closest, relatively cheap bar. Is my bro not out with you tonight?"

"I'm afraid we've lost him a little." Scott raised his eyebrows and shrugged resignedly although still smiling. "He's out with Pam. It seems he's quite taken with her."

Tabitha felt a surge of glee. "Well that's so wonderful, I'm well chuffed about them two. They just seem so…."

Suddenly remembering that she wasn't just having a conversation with Scott but was actually gushing in front of a bunch of lads, she regained her composure.

"Anyway have a good night whatever you get up to. Nice to see you." Tabitha turned to head back indoors to her fate.

Scott stood and watched as Peter guided Tabitha back into the pub, hoping that this guy would treat her better than that last piece of work.

"You alright there Scotty boy? You can stop staring now", his friend joshed.

Scott laughed. "Ah hey, don't be mad mate. She's George's kid sister init. I've known her forever. Behave yerself."

Tabitha and Peter walked back into the bar so slowly that they were almost tripping over each other. They spotted Marnie and Kelly chatting to a group of musicians excitedly. Kelly jumped up and down when she saw them and beckoned them to come over.

" Hey guys", Marnie squealed. "We've got an in. These lovely gents have some spare percussion…um..things and they said that we can play with them."

Tabitha stifled a giggle.

Kelly gave Tabitha a 'pack it in' look but Marnie carried on, unaware of what she had said to amuse Tabitha.

"I'm afraid we are one instrument short though so you'll have to decide amongst yourselves who wants to join in and play the triangle."

Tabitha and Peter burst out laughing at the situation that they had somehow found themselves in, leaving the band looking a little confused and dismayed.

"Oh my god, we don't mean any offence guys", pleaded Peter. "My friend and I just aren't very talented."

"Like, at all", Tabitha backed him up.

The band looked a little less hurt now and Peter made a huge effort to hold his serious face for the sake of relations with their new friends. "I do feel that I should do the gentlemanly thing here and step aside and let Tabitha play the triangle."

Tabitha poked him in the kidney surreptitiously. "Ah thanks Peter and thank you guys for trusting me with your..um...triangle. I think that more drinks may be in order."

So it transpired that Tabitha's day ended very differently to how it had started. Whilst boosting her professional career this morning, she had not pictured that nine hours later she would be learning a completely new skill. It was another beautiful reminder that you never know what is just around the corner and more importantly, a valuable lesson to check the pub's event board before heading out.

That night Tabitha resolved for the sake of all humanity, to never be drunk, in charge of a percussion instrument ever again.

CHAPTER ELEVEN

"Oh my God Pam, I wish you'd been there to see it", Tabitha chuckled down the phone the next day. "I felt a bit guilty really. Those boys were a serious band and we were quite awful. At the beginning anyway. I think we might have got better."

Pam laughed. "Did you actually get better or just drunker? Anyway, I bet you looked good up there hon, it sounds like they would have just enjoyed having some pretty girls jamming with them. After all, who brings spare percussion instruments out with them if they're not looking for some action."

Tabitha nearly choked on her cornflakes. "Crikey. Is that how it's done these days? I thought diamonds were a girl's best friend but well, I guess tambourines and things could be a good softener too. Anyway how was your night with George...without unnecessary details please?"

"Really cool thanks hon. Your brother actually is a diamond. Don't tell him I said that though. Anyway, that's why I called. He asked if I wanted to go to the Speedway this evening but I said I wanted to see you so he suggested that maybe we could go as a group. It's totes up to you though."

Tabitha did a quick mental check of her finances and her hangover. "Ya know, that sounds great. It'll be fun to do something different and George picks on me less when you're around, always has, even before you were, well....you know."

Pam laughed. "Ah, your brother is always lovely. He's just totes adorbs. He makes me feel so...."

Tabitha realised that Pam was just trying to make her cringe now and she obligingly made a fake retching noise. "Shout me later when you have a plan, you weirdo", she signed off.

As Tabitha hung up, she chuckled again at Pam's 'looking for some action' presumption. She wondered if the boys from the band last night had been interested in any of them. Had she forgotten how to recognise the signs? She hadn't actually been with Gary for so long that she shouldn't remember them but she had thought that it was going to last forever so maybe she'd just shut that part of her brain down.

It was probably a good thing for now anyway. She had enough to keep her occupied with work and having fun with her friends. The last thing she needed right now was a new complication. And how would she even be able to trust somebody again after what Gary had done to her? She'd been completely unaware that there had even been an issue. She still had her tan from their beautiful holiday together for goodness sake but it couldn't be more over.

Snuggles looked up from her lap as if sensing her sudden sadness. She felt the intended comfort from his concern and gently stroked the fur between his eyes, smiling fondly as it sent him off to sleep. Well, now she couldn't really move and disturb her dear furry buddy so she may as well just chill here for a bit.

She flicked through the tv channels. News, nope, not ready for that yet today. Loud people cooking, cooking fish of all things, at this time of day, um definitely not. Friends? Yes, she had a winner. She'd only seen this episode about seventeen times so it was worth another watch of course.

She soon got lost in it and found herself beaming at her tv besties from across the pond. "She's your Lobster", she proclaimed joyfully, in time with Phoebe.

Gary hadn't liked Friends. He thought it was Juvenile. Well sod Gary. She made a pledge to herself right now to never again be with a man who didn't like Friends. Nobody was coming into her tank unless they wanted to hold claws with her and watch repeated episodes of Friends forevermore.

That evening Tabitha, Pam and George clambered up to the top deck of the Speedway shuttle bus.

"So, what did you do with your well-deserved rest day Tabby?" enquired Pam. "Next to nothing I hope."

"I can confirm that a very enjoyable next to nothing day was undertaken", Tabitha grinned, not feeling even a little guilty. "I sat and watched three episodes of Friends back to back before having a nice long bath. Guess which episode I started on?" Tabitha imitated Lobster claws.

"She's your Lobster", came a voice from behind them. The girls both looked around at George.

"It weren't me". George shook his head. "I have no idea what you're both talking about."

Scott headed to join them from further back on the bus and sat down next to George. "Hey guys, sorry, I wasn't hiding. I was just finishing an email." His neck flushed red now as he gave a resigned shrug and repeated, "'She's your Lobster', I love that episode too. Can't deny it." He looked back down at his phone to signal that an opinion from George was not invited.

As the bus pulled up outside the stadium, the group joined the throng of fans heading in through the large gates. Glorious smells swirled through the air from the food vans and excited chatter competed with the rock music blaring out through the tannoy. George bought a couple of programmes and pulled some pens out of his jacket pocket.

"We can keep up with the scoring in here. We should get some bets put on too if you're feeling lucky ladies." He grinned at Pam who looked as if she already felt like the luckiest girl on the planet right now.

Scott took one of the programs and opened it to show Tabitha who he thought was worth putting some cash on.

She smiled as she saw a couple of names who just had to be Swedish.

She had come to the speedway a few times as a youngster and at the age of nine had developed quite a crush on a gorgeous Swedish rider who was a home team favourite. She'd often daydreamed of her beautiful hero falling from his bike and her running across the track to stroke his blonde curls back from his disappointed brow. His dismay at losing the race would dissipate as he looked up at his angelic helper. Not quite your Disney Princess fairy tale stuff but romantic all the same.

She looked around now at the heaving stands and couldn't believe that she had waited so long to return here as an adult. There was such a fantastic buzz around. The home team were being introduced to the crowd now whilst being driven around the track in an open backed truck. Air horns sounded and people roared their support at their racers.

"Let's go and put some bets on now", enthused Tabitha, "and get some beers". She looked around excitedly to see if the bar was still in the same place. "And let's get some chips with the little wooden fork thingies."

The other three all laughed at her eagerness. George was so relieved that his little sister had got her mojo back now that she was free of that stuck up idiot she had been knocking about with for the past year.

Scott gallantly offered his arm and escorted Tabitha to the bar where they ordered four pints of their finest cheap lager.

"So how was your night last night?" Scott asked politely. "You looked like you were having fun."

"Yeah it was awesome. A few of us ended up joining in with the open mic night which was a new experience for me. Not something I'll be rushing to repeat though." Tabitha added, giggling at the memory. "Did you have a good one?"

"Yeah it was alright, cheers." Scott looked thoughtful. "And um, what was your friend's name? Peter?"

"Yes, that's right. He's hilarious."

"Ah that's great. So is he a potential suitor, do you think?"

Tabitha nearly choked on her drink and then felt bad as Scott looked a little taken aback.

"Sorry Scott. I didn't mean to laugh. It's just that Peter is very happily married and well, as far as relationships, I'm not sure I'll be rushing straight back into anything."

"Oh ok. Right. I see. We best get a wiggle on if we want to get a bet on the first race."

The night was everything and more than Tabitha could have hoped for and she even came out of the stadium with more money than she went in with which was a tremendous shock to all of them. She was well known for her awful luck when gambling usually. In fact her lack of talent for gambling actually made her triangle skills look sublime.

She soon began to get used to her best friend and brother being an item, helped along by the fact that every race win was sealed with a kiss, even when the win wasn't by the rider they had bet on, and eventually even when the rider wasn't actually a member of their own team. She had never seen her brother so open with his pdas. She was so happy for them and it helped that she was comfortable in Scott's company too. He was a perfect gentleman and good fun, especially now that his nerves seemed to be subsiding a little around her lately.

By the time they were all on the bus home, Tabitha was blissfully tired from laughing and cheering. She leant against the window and peered out at the bright moon. Just one short week ago her world had fallen apart and she had wanted to just shut down all of her senses and hide away. Now, so much crazy stuff had happened and she felt alive as she relished the memories made tonight, the smell of the bikes still fresh and her ears ringing from the closing firework display.

She offered up a prayer of thanks for the strength that she now felt but she also realised that she could take some of the credit herself.

CHAPTER TWELVE

Tabitha's boss had not been wrong when she'd warned her that she was going to be a very busy girl. The following weeks blurred into a frenzy of meetings, conference calls and hours of brainstorming. Tabitha was delighted how her plans were being received and put into reality though. Some very well-known people had jumped at the chance to be involved in the project.

Filming had already begun around various parts of the world. After another full day at the Yerans offices, Tabitha was delighted to receive an invite to join the team in Paris at the end of the year where some of the adverts would be being filmed.

She had tried to remain in control of herself as she'd gratefully accepted the invite but she couldn't help but do a little hop and skip later as she headed out into the fresh evening air.

It was getting dark early now so it was easy to lose track of time and Tabitha was surprised to see a message from Pam asking where she was. She felt so lucky to be in a job where she wasn't clockwatching in the least but knew that she'd better get a shift on now or she would be in danger of being teased for forgetting that the weekend had officially started a couple of hours ago for most normal people.

Pam's uncle Simon was in a rock band who were playing a show tonight at a pub in the next town. Realising what the time actually was, Tabitha ran past the bus stop to the taxi rank, deciding that she deserved to spoil herself a little anyway.

As her cab pulled up outside the Bell Tavern, Tabitha could hear the music already blasting out. Maybe this was just what she needed to get her out of work mode and straight into the weekend spirit.

She had to admit that deep down she had been a little bit hesitant when Pam had told her about the show as she didn't know what to expect but she soon noticed as she headed inside that the place was full to the rafters of people of all ages and appearances and also that she immediately felt comfortable amongst the enthusiastic crowd.

She headed into the bouncing throng of fans, searching for Pam, smiling warmly at a lady who was gleefully flashing a Baby on board t-shirt to her friends.

Failing to find Pam, she decided to aim for the bar to get a drink and send her a text. She turned around startled as she suddenly felt somebody take hold of her hand. She looked along the attached arm to find Scott grinning at her from amongst the huddle of bodies. She hadn't known he was going to be here but she felt really happy to see him.

"Hey Tabs, What are you having?" he shouted, still holding her hand as if it would make it easier for them to hear each other. Tabitha called her request over to him and waited as he got served, finding herself already tapping her foot along to the band. As they headed over to find the others Scott shouted over the music, "These guys are really awesome", just as the song finished. The pair of them laughed loudly, relieved that the ensuing cheering saved Scott from too much embarrassment.

Pam had managed to get quite a crowd along and everybody looked like they were having a great time.

Tabitha handed one of the pints from Scott to her brother and casually licked her arm where her giggling had caused a spillage.

"Hey classy bird", laughed Pam, hugging her friend. "It's about time you got here, you workaholic. You have some catching up to do."

"Oh, if you insist", laughed Tabitha, taking a large sip of her drink.

Scott looked her up and down and nodded in approval. "Look at you. You look dead smart Tabby", he said. "Kind of like....Clueless."

"What?" Tabitha and Pam burst out laughing.

"I mean, oh you know....that film where she's all smart."

"Oh I see, the film, Clueless", giggled Tabitha, trying to pull a straight face as Scott blushed. "Thanks Scott. That's very kind."

George managed to save the moment as he rubbed his knuckles on the top of Tabitha's head and blurted out. "Nah mate. She just looks clueless. All the time."

The drinks flowed and the songs kept coming. Tabitha was excited to find that she knew most of the tunes, with them conveniently being a mixture of both her and her Mum's music collections. The crowd all jumped and swayed and sang along and she even spotted some air drumming, which she knew was a good sign of a band being well appreciated.

In one break between songs, the drummer stood up, acknowledging the approval of the crowd. He raised his sticks in the air and the crowd roared as if they were being conducted. Tabitha looked around her gleefully and savoured the elevated atmosphere, noting that this was definitely something that she should do more often.

"Thanks guys. This next song is a little cover we've been working on. This arrangement was my idea so if it's pants you can blame me. I'd like to dedicate this to the lady I love, Sarah. Love you babe and you do look wonderful tonight."

Tabitha joined the rest of the crowd in following the pointed drumstick to where a delighted but slightly embarrassed looking lady stood. The room erupted into cheers and Tabitha felt her cheeks almost hurt as she smiled broadly, feeling absolute delight for a complete stranger called Sarah. That's how I want to be loved, she thought to herself, noting that she would have had more chance of winning the lottery than ever seeing Gary make such a bold statement for her.

She realised for certain at that moment that she really was well rid of Gary, and not just because of what had happened at the end. It wasn't just an empty soundbite that people had been repeatedly saying to her after the breakup. They all actually had a point. It wasn't that she hadn't been enough to match up to his expectations. It was that she was too much for him. She never could be the person to just fit into his world. She had her own fabulous world and she deserved so much better.

Tabitha suddenly realised that as she was thinking, she was still staring at Sarah with an inane grin on her face and turned away quickly to find Scott looking at her quizzically. "You alright there Tabby?"

"Yes thanks", she laughed, "I most certainly am my dear".

CHAPTER THIRTEEN

"Oh Mum", exclaimed Tabitha excitedly into her phone. "I do believe that Bath at Christmas time just might be the most magical place ever."

"Darling, that's wonderful. I'm just so pleased that you've been able to go to Marnie's hen weekend after all now that you're in charge of your own calendar. Do you know many people there?"

"Yeah. Kelly and Lizzie from the office are both here and Marnie's gang are all so much fun. Her cousin is cerrazy and reckons she has a surprise stripper turning up when we least expect it over the weekend."

"Oh crikey dear. Well, please be careful where he swings his bits and pieces. There was this one time when I…"

"Muuum!", Tabitha squealed. "Do I really want to hear this?"

There was a slight pause from her Mother. "Yeah, maybe not, actually love. So anyway, as you were saying..the Christmas market is lovely, yeah?"

"Yes Mum. We'll defo have to come here together another year. Anyway I'd better get going. We have a comedy club followed by a disco tonight then a spa and afternoon tea tomorrow."

"Wow it sounds like a great amount of organising has gone into this. I'm rather jealous. Just don't go drinking too much tonight and ruining tomorrow. You know you're a lightweight."

"Ha ha. Yes Mummy. Love you, bye."

After Tabitha had signed off, she rummaged through her suitcase for her dress. She noted that maybe she should have hung it up earlier as now she was definitely going to have to iron it. It was all well and good that she was in charge of her own destiny now but she could actually do with a little nudge in the right direction occasionally if she was totally honest.

Tonight was also Gary's company's Christmas Ball. That was why when Marnie had invited Tabitha to Bath this weekend, despite it being months in advance, she'd felt that she'd had to say no just in case it had clashed. As it happened it was clashing but it no longer mattered.

An hour and a rainforest shower later, Tabitha applied the finishing touch to her look with a holly red lipstick that Gary would definitely not have approved of her wearing. It would be fine on other girls perhaps but a little tarty for his own girlfriend. Tabitha looked herself up and down in the mirror before leaving to meet the others in the foyer. Yes, she scrubbed up alright, she decided gleefully. She gave herself a wink and headed out, giggling to herself.

As the sixteen girls bundled into the comedy club they were greeted warmly. "So you, my dear, must be the beautiful bride." A smart elderly gentleman, who appeared as though he may have been here for as long as the building had, took Marnie by the elbow. "Are you certain you want to be getting wedded off and don't want to just run away with me?"

Marnie played along and looked thoughtful. "Oh well, now I do seem to have found myself in a bit of a pickle Sir."

Their host beamed his approval at her witty comeback and led them to their tables right in front of the stage.

"Oh blimey", muttered Lizzie. "We're gonna be right under the comedians' noses. That means we're in for trouble, especially the amount of times I have to go for a pee."

"There's only one thing for it", Kelly declared resolutely as she picked up the drinks menu. "Well, two things actually I suppose. We either hardly drink at all so we don't have to go and wee or we drink so much that we won't care if we get singled out."

The fact that she was browsing the menu like the words might fade if she didn't read it quickly enough showed her preference. As Marnie's sister ordered three jugs of cocktails for each table, the ladies decided that it was actually beyond their control and just pure fabulous fate that the latter option was chosen.

Tabitha looked around and took in the joyful atmosphere in the room and once again was so delighted that she was here. How could she have even considered missing this.

What Tabitha didn't know was that Gary had attended his work Christmas ball with his new girlfriend Vanessa, only to find his now ex girlfriend Vanessa making out with his now ex friend Steve in the cloakroom!

The following day the girls hid a multitude of sins behind their sunglasses as they sat in the beautiful tearooms. Tabitha was grateful for the habit that her Mother had instilled in her to drink lots of water whilst drinking alcohol. Every time that she had visited the loo, she had also stopped off at the water cooler. This had meant that she had needed to go to the loo more of course but they had got off pretty lightly with the comedians' banter. There were other hen party groups at the show so they hadn't been picked on too much, except for poor Marnie.

She'd got a bit of stick once as she'd gone out to the loo in her veil. The stand up had stopped speaking and just stared at her, causing the whole room to fall silent and also look at Marnie who was none the wiser and trying to tiptoe between tables without blocking the view or disturbing anybody.

She had gradually realised that all eyes were on her and had turned slowly back to look at the stage with a petrified look on her face. The comedian was delighted with this opportunity and asked what Marnie thought she was going to do if she needed a wee during her ceremony.

"Would you just get up and walk out then too? I know, I'll pretend I'm the vicar and just wait for you to come back. At least then we can work out the timings for the day properly. Make sure your vol au vents don't get cold. Nobody likes a chilly vol au vent, ain't that right ladies?" she'd added as she'd sat down on the stage floor and looked at her watch.

Marnie, for a minute, looked like she didn't know whether to keep walking out or come back before the comedian burst into laughter and told her, "Bugger off girl, if I make you wee I'll have to clean it up after. Yes, people. I'm also the cleaner here. I'm multi-talented init". She spread her arms and bowed her head, inviting praise from the crowd. " No seriously", she continued, "these gigs ain't making me that much you know! Besides dear". She'd looked back at Marnie. "I'm getting on a bit. By the time I get back up off this floor, you'll have finished having your hover wee and be back, oh yes, do hover, I wouldn't sit down on those seats girls!" With that, the comedian had scratched herself furiously, the crowd had erupted into laughter and Marnie had made her exit.

Today the girls found that they were in the perfect place for recovery as there was an endless assortment of teas on hand with all kinds of healing powers. A string quartet played up on the stage, creating a delightfully relaxing ambience. Tabitha hoped beyond hopes that Marnie's cousin's stripper wouldn't be turning up now. There were ladies across the room with wide brimmed hats who looked like they may well come here every weekend to meet with their friends and have a catch up on the events of society. She felt that their society probably didn't include oiled up young men gyrating over lunch, but maybe she shouldn't assume, she thought, then realised that she was now staring a little impolitely and returned her attention to her own table.

Tabitha concluded that she personally definitely had the best of both worlds, to be able to enjoy a packet of pork scratchings down the local as well as to indulge in these fluffy scones and simply delectable sandwiches with the crusts cut off. She wondered what they did with the crusts. Then she wondered if anybody else was wondering. She acknowledged that maybe she was a bit of an overthinker sometimes whilst also wondering whether if she mentioned it, would other people also begin to wonder. It was nice to have the time to just wonder about wondering anyway, she decided.

The blissful day continued as they headed to the spa later that afternoon. As Tabitha floated in the heated rooftop pool, gazing up at the hazy winter sun she made a vow to herself that she really would make the time to do things like this more often. Forgetting to look at the time whilst working was one thing but not knowing the time due to absolute relaxation, well that was something that she could definitely get used to.

She could get somewhere close to this feeling whilst listening to her guided meditation pieces but why just meditate and pretend to be somewhere else when you could actually be at those places in real life. Yes, pinky promise to self, she thought dreamily, do this again and often.

Tabitha let the salt in the water take her weight as she closed her eyes, feeling completely zen. She allowed her ears to be submerged so that the sounds around her faded and she felt like she was floating through space, all alone in infinity, spectacularly free in the universe, just drifting along aimlessly, until, bump, collision, gulp, water, cough, splutter, come to standing, rub eyes, regain breath and then ooh.

The bumper or the bumpee turned out to be a tall, bronzed adonis. How had she not noticed him before? His fair hair sparkled like gold in the sunlight and his blue eyes stared into hers, full of concern.

"Are you ok there Miss?" he drawled dreamily. Ah American, Tabitha realised. From the South, she thought. Mmm, maybe a cowboy, she fantasised.

She realised that she was just looking at him and not actually speaking. She interrupted her private conversation with herself to answer the handsome stranger. "Oh I'm fine, thank you. I'm really sorry. I was just miles away."

"As was I. I think it was my fault that I bumped you."

Tabitha battled a smirk. "I had my eyes closed so I think we just happened to bump each other." Are we flirting?, she wondered..

The adonis grinned now and became even more stupendously gorgeous.

Wow, thought Tabitha. So this is it. I do still know how to read the signs. There is definitely something going on here. We're absolutely flirting.

"So what brings you here?" she enquired. "Are you visiting Bath or do you live here?"

She hoped that she didn't sound too forward.

He took a breath to respond and Tabitha prayed that his answer wouldn't be that he was just visiting the UK and returning home imminently.

"I'm visiting my sister in-law who lives here in Bath. Such a beautiful place. How about you?"

Ouch thought Tabitha, In-laws, that's a nuisance. That means he's already been snatched up. Bloomin' married. How inconvenient.

"Ah how lovely", she fibbed. "Yes it truly is a beautiful city. I'm here with some friends for a hen weekend."

"Awesome. Well it was nice to meet you. To bump into you", he laughed (and angels cried at the beautiful sound).

As he swam away, Tabitha shook her head. Well how wrong was she about the signs? The adonis wasn't flirting.

He was just being friendly and jovial. Maybe she needed to find a guidebook or something about the dating world. Anyway, she was pleased that she had at least been interested. That was a positive start at least to her recovery and future romantic career.

Tabitha noticed that her fingers were beginning to look rather wrinkly and headed for the edge of the pool just as Lizzie and Kelly wandered out of the building.

"Cor, it's a bit nippy up here", shivered Kelly. "Aren't you freezing Tabby?"

"No, it's perfect in here, girls. you should defo get in. It's fine…."

"….once you're in", they all finished in unison, laughing at the saying that seemed to grace every holiday ever, especially at home in Britain.

"Anyway I'm going for a steam now I reckon", Tabitha pulled herself up to standing against the weight of the salt water. "A little detox would be good. Hey girls? What…?"

Tabitha was confused and a little offended to see that she had lost both of the girl's attention as they stared over her shoulder. She looked round quizzically and her heart skipped a beat or two as she saw Adonis standing closely behind her.

"Um so, I beg your pardon for intruding Miss but I didn't get your name".

"Tabitha. I'm Tabitha and um."

"Billy". He held out a big strong hand and gently shook Tabitha's hand which felt lost but safe inside it.

Of course he was called Billy. Billy the kid. Mmm Billy the gorgeous cowboy. Tabitha turned to the girls and Lizzie gestured with her eyes that Tabitha should be speaking to Billy some more immediately and certainly not be looking back at them.

"So Tabitha, I was wondering if you would be around long enough to maybe grab a drink with me tonight? I feel bad about bumping you earlier."

"Um, well thank you for asking but I need to be up pretty early tomorrow to travel back home. I have an early meeting you see..."

"I can postpone that", Lizzie piped up instantly. "We can do it Tuesday instead. That works better for me anyway."

Tabitha turned to see Lizzie nodding decisively and realised that she didn't really have a say in that. Kelly looked like she was physically unable to blink as she watched the situation unfold.

"Well yes, I suppose I could, if that's ok with everyone else. We're having dinner together but then….um…I assume..um..will your wife be joining us?" Tabitha had just fallen foul of a cheating man. She was certainly not going to be playing any part in breaking somebody else's heart.

"My wife?" exclaimed Adonis, apparently known in the human world as Billy. "Oh I'm not married Miss."

"Oh you said you were visiting your sister in-law. I just thought….."

Adonis put his hand to his forehead. "Oh no. Oh I'm such a duffus. I should have made sure to explain. My sister in-law is my brother's wife. He's away with the Air Force at the moment so I check in on her and the kids as often as I can whilst I'm over here in the UK."

Oh how divine, Tabitha thought. Talk about a swing of emotions. Instead of being married, he was single and kind and thoughtful and had she mentioned, gorgeous?

Tabitha looked at the girls who now looked like they might shake her if she didn't seal the deal.

"Yes then. That would be really nice. We're having dinner at The Coopers Arms in Milsom street so maybe I could meet you there in the bar afterwards at about 9pm if that's not too late?"

Billy's eyes sparkled as he grinned broadly. "That is more than perfect, Tabitha. I have a little work to do later so that will be great timing".

He climbed out of the pool and the girls shamelessly gawped at his bronzed toned body.

"Ok that's enough now girls", Tabitha laughed. "Imagine how we must look. How would it look if three guys were staring at a girl like this?"

"Yeah alright spoilsport. You have a point", laughed Lizzie whilst grabbing one last sneaky peak.

"Anyway", Tabitha beamed. "I'm off for a steam and a sauna then I just might need to buy a new dress as I think I have a date, you know."

CHAPTER FOURTEEN

The girls were ushered into a private dining room when they arrived at the restaurant that evening. Tabitha wore her new dress in midnight blue, daringly paired with new red shoes. She felt rather marvellous after a lovely detox in the steam room earlier and a cheeky shot of tequila with the ladies before leaving the hotel.

It was quite apparent that the group were now nearing the end of their weekend away. A comfortable calm encompassed the ladies as they ate together. They reflected on all the fun that they'd had on the trip and enthused about Marnie's impending nuptials. Dinner was delicious and Tabitha was relieved to find that she was starving, despite her date nerves and the Cream tea this afternoon. It seemed that a swim in the fresh air was very good for creating a healthy appetite and this food was well worth forgetting to count calories for.

As their empty plates were cleared away, Tabitha sat back contentedly and listened to what she guessed would be described as lift music which had been playing in the background with some very different versions of well known songs. She'd had no idea that you could create a mellow version of Cotton eyed Joe. As the tune faded out she wondered what could possibly come next. The ketchup song maybe, she joked to herself.

Ah no, it was in fact the theme to The Good, the bad and the ugly. Of course. Another interesting choice for dining music. And it was getting increasingly louder. How very strange. Just then the lights flickered on and off before dimming down low and a blue spotlight shone out from the corner of the room, just as a door that Tabitha hadn't noticed before slowly opened.

The girls all looked around, a little bewildered, as a cowboy boot extended around the door followed by a long leather-clad leg, then the rest of what was evidently Marnie's surprise strippergram.

They all gasped in a combination of shock and delight as poor Marnie looked as though she might well faint. Oh well, her cousin had warned her, but now that it was nearly hometime it appeared that she thought that maybe she'd got away with it.

The cowboy swaggered seductively across the room, his face hidden in the shadow of his Stetson hat as he made his way over to Marnie.

He removed a matchstick from the corner of his mouth and whispered huskily. "Well ma'am, that was quite a ride. I can't wait to get out of these clothes. I feel soooo dirty."

The girls screamed with joy and Tabitha wondered for just a second what the diners out in the main restaurant must be thinking. She felt for her dear friend but thankfully Marnie looked like she had resigned herself to her fate now as she sat up tall in her seat with an amused grin on her face. If it was going to happen then she may as well enjoy it.

As it was, their cowboy was reasonably tasteful. There was some clever lasso work carried out whilst gyrating at a polite distance away from Marnie. Once he had stripped down to just his underwear and hat, Tabitha wondered which was coming off next. She was relieved for Marnie that the underwear stayed on but her mouth fell wide open as the hat was slowly removed and placed gently on top of Marnie's head. Oh my god, it was only bloody Billy from the pool. Billy the damn kid as she had named him in her imagination. He actually was a cowboy after all and a stripping one at that and..good gracious..her date in about forty five minutes.

Kelly quickly recognised him too and looked as if she might burst as she tried to continue to watch Billy's performance and also take photos of both Marnie and Tabitha's faces simultaneously. Tabitha couldn't believe it. Had he seen her? Had he known that she was going to be here? Well she had said that this was where they were going to be eating and he had said that that was 'more than perfect'.

He bowed with his hat now held tightly to his chest, bidding farewell to the bride to be.

He gently kissed Marnie's hand, put his hat back on and strode confidently back around the table. As he got to Tabitha's seat, he paused, tipped his hat to her, gave her a wink and left the room.

The waitress reappeared as the lights went back up and the lift music resumed. "Well that made my shift a lot more exciting. Is everybody ready for dessert?"

An hour later Tabitha walked into the bar after promising the girls that she would not go anywhere else with 'the stripper' without messaging them to let them know what she was doing. She realised that this was partly for her safety but mostly for the girl's insatiable appetites for gossip and information about the gorgeous cowboy.

She didn't really know what to look out for now. So far she had only seen Billy in his swimming trunks and then in a Cowboy outfit which had been gradually reduced to his underwear. She was relieved to spot him sitting at the bar, appropriately dressed in jeans and a polo shirt. She noted how nicely his long legs filled those jeans.

"Howdy cowboy", she said quietly as she approached the bar.

Billy stood up to greet her and pulled out a bar chair for her.

"I'm sorry I'm a little late," Tabitha continued. "Dinner went a little off schedule."

Billy's face broke into a huge grin. "Well, for that I think the apology is all mine Miss."

Tabitha felt relieved that at least they had a useful conversation starter.

"So about that. How did you get into...I mean how long have you...I mean um do you enjoy..?

"Stripping", laughed Billy. "Yeah, it's great fun. As far as customer service roles go, this is rather easy. You don't get complaints and there aren't many rules".

"Mmm I suppose not", Tabitha giggled.

"Mostly it's a more enjoyable way to earn some extra money while I'm at University, than the bar work I'd been doing at the local 'Spoons' pub. No offence to the old boy regulars there of course."

Tabitha felt a wave of panic at the word University, suddenly concerned that she may be visiting Cougar town by accident but was thankful to learn that Billy was only a year younger than her, at twenty four. He had finished the third year of his law degree back home in Virginia and had jumped at the opportunity to go on an exchange for a year at The University of London so that he could study UK law as a comparison.

Tabitha told him all about her job. They talked about their families, the friends that Billy missed back home and his niece and nephew that he had the opportunity to see more of while he was here in the UK. She found it so easy to talk to him. Anybody that saw them would have thought they'd known each other for years. Time flew by and before they knew it the bartender called last orders.

Tabitha admitted that she probably shouldn't have any more to drink. She was disappointed that the night was coming to an end though.

"I guess it is late and your friends will be glad to see you back safely."

Mmm, Yes and no, thought Tabitha knowingly.

Can I walk you back to your hotel? I need to have a sneaky smoke before I get back to my brother's anyway so it's sure no bother."

"That'd be lovely. Thank you Billy. I don't approve of the smoking though, young man."

Billy laughed and offered her his arm as they walked out of the restaurant. It felt comfortable. Tabitha wondered if maybe too much though, kind of beyond dating material. Had she made the awful mistake of managing to friend zone this gorgeous specimen of a man? How upsetting. She wondered if he felt the same. Maybe it was her self protection kicking in. After all, he was only going to be in England for another 5 months.

When they arrived at her hotel, Tabitha reached into her bag to get her door key ready. "Well thank you Billy. It's been so nice to meet you."

"Likewise Tabitha. I'm mighty glad that I bumped you this afternoon."

"Well I guess I'll be.."

"Would it be forward of me to ask if I could call you?" Billy blurted and he looked awkward for the first time since they'd met. "Or you could take my number if you prefer and then you can decide."

"That'd be cool. My mobile's on here." Tabitha took her Perfect promos business card from the pocket of her purse and passed it to Billy. Then, wondering if they should kiss or not, and how much, she reached up and kissed him gently in a one side of the mouth type thing. She wasn't quite sure what that meant and he probably wasn't either but to some extent she was back in the game.

She felt herself blushing. "Goodnight Billy."

"Goodnight Miss."

CHAPTER FIFTEEN

"Oh my goodness Tabby. So you actually snogged the stripper?"

"No Mum", Tabitha squealed. "It wasn't like that and when I first met him I didn't even know he was the stripper, a stripper. I mean he's not just a stripper you know. Did you only listen to the rude bits?"

Tabitha and her Mum hadn't even touched their dinners yet as they caught up on the excitement of the weekend away.

George and Scott, however, disgusted by the teatime conversation, frantically wolfed down their meatballs as if they were pool balls needing to be cleared from the table as quickly as possible.

"So anyway", George interrupted dramatically. "I've actually got some news too."

Tabitha and her Mum stopped their conversation abruptly and looked at George, his face full of excitement.

Ooh could it be news about him and Pam? Ah maybe not, it was a bit soon for any big news? Maybe something to do with work then? George beamed at the group one at a time, building up the anticipation"

Well, come on then", Mum pushed. "We're waiting."

George looked serious. "It's just that. Um. Well….I need to let you all know that….I have a nice new spot coming out on my chin!"

"Ah George", Tabitha wailed and flicked a pea at her brother's head. "What the heck?"

"Well jeez, someone needs to stop you two. It's disgusting talking about strippers at the dinner table. Where's your decency?"

Tabitha shook her head. "Oh but talking about zits is ok?"

"That's enough, the pair of you", Mum interjected. "Looks like you kids are washing up again."

Scott laughed as he wiped his plate with his finger.

"Don't worry Scotty boy. I'll find something for you to do in the garden for me. You can all earn your dinner."

Tabitha and George rejoined forces to grin at Scott, now that he had also been told off.

After a lovely evening and with chores completed, Tabitha walked home full and happy. Her Mother had shooed her off before it got dark after she refused lifts from the boys. "A summer body is made in the winter you know", she had stated matter of factly, repeating a meme that had inspired her hugely, all of two days ago.

Tabitha pulled her jacket around her tightly as the cool evening air gently swirled about her. She looked up at the sky as stars began to appear and she thanked them. Everything was working out perfectly. She'd had a few crazy weeks at work but had loved it and she was gradually finding the perfect balance now between her career and spending time with her friends and loved ones. She felt on top of everything and was loving it. She wasn't sure if she had ever felt as in control of her life as she did right now. It was so good that it actually felt too good to be true.

And apparently it was too good to be true.

Tabitha's stomach did a somersault as she spotted a much too familiar car sitting in her driveway.

Responding to a mixture of inbuilt good manners and absolute shock, Tabitha soon found herself sitting at her kitchen table, drinking a cup of tea with Gary.

It didn't take long for him to pour out his sob story about Vanessa and Steve and how blindsided he had been. She was surprised how somebody who could be so judgemental of other people's manners had missed out the part where he asked her how she was, but then how could this man surprise her any more than he already had.

Tabitha nodded repeatedly and made all the right noises as he carried on about what a cheating pig Steve was. She tried to look through him, past him, anything but at him, as she annoyingly felt her heart softening for his pain. After all she had loved this man.

What did he want from her though? How could he come here of all places for sympathy? He suddenly reached across the table and took her hand in his, shaking his head forlornly. He stared into her eyes and she felt her knees begin to tremble. She bit her lip as he took a slow deep breath before speaking again.

"I know how you must have felt now Tabitha and I'm so sorry for what I did to you." He lifted her hand and kissed it. " I just wish things could go back to how they were. I'm so sad and lonely."

Tabitha suddenly felt as if she was having an out of body experience. She hadn't expected to see him again, yet alone hear him admit out loud that he had regrets. He wanted things to go back to how they were?

The room span. She wanted to hold him. She wanted to forget all about Vanessa and kiss the sorrow from his face. Yes, ok, maybe she wanted to go back to how things were too, well mostly how they were, but could they really do that now? As her mind raced, she looked down at their entwined hands on the table. They fitted together so perfectly. It was just meant to be.

Gary shook his head again before continuing, "I just wish she still loved me. I want her back. How can I get her back Tabs?"

Tabitha felt as if her heart was going to break all over again as, with a thud, the realisation hit her that his sadness was for Vanessa. He wanted him and Vanessa to go back to how they were, not she and him.

She fought to catch her breath and then suddenly she felt as though she was somehow channelling the dear people that cared about her all at once as fury bubbled up in her.

Her sadness evaporated as she beheld the final disrespect that this man was now showing to her.

She stood up from the table, her chair flying to the floor as she did so. Gary looked shocked. His reaction made her even crosser. The fact that he couldn't even understand why she was angry made her blood boil.

"Get out", she managed to say calmly as she dug her nails into the palm of her hand.

"What? But Tabitha? You're the first person that I thought of, I mean, I didn't know who else I could talk to about this. Cos, well, you know Steve. I obviously can't exactly talk to him about it. And my Mother doesn't really like Vanessa. You know, she liked you so much and.."

Tabitha marched to the front door and held it open wide. "You are not welcome here Gary. Now if you don't mind, I have things to be getting on with."

Gary's continued unawareness of his audacity confirmed so much for Tabitha. This was not a man that she could have spent her life with. Thank goodness for Vanessa and his wandering eye.

As he walked past her and out of the door mournfully, Tabitha patted him gently on the shoulder. "I hope everything works out for you", she said truthfully.

She gently closed the door behind him and leant against it, breathing deeply. Snuggles poked his head around the living room door to see if everything was ok. Tabitha smiled at her little friend and, sensing that all was actually well now, he strutted nonchalantly off to his food bowl meowing, pointing out that he now needed to be promoted back to being Tabitha's number one concern.

CHAPTER SIXTEEN

Pam and Laura sat opposite Tabitha in The Shetlands with their mouths wide open in amazement at Gary's latest stunt.

"Good god", exclaimed Laura. "Some of the things that my kids come out with baffle me but that man is really something else. What do they say? You can't teach stupid!"

"He really is the git that keeps on giving", agreed Pam, her cheeks flushed from anger, as well as from her rhubarb gin.

Tabitha laughed. "The git that keeps on giving! That's really good Pammy. Do you fancy a job in advertising?"

Pam shook her head. "Well I'm pleased you seem to be ok at least. I could throttle that guy. Ooh if I ever set eyes on him around here."

Tabitha looked around their dear old local and concluded that she probably wouldn't.

"Anyway!" She decided that enough of their precious time had been spent talking about Gary. "What have I missed with you two? Anything I should know? More babies on the horizon Laura? Pam, I hope my brother is still behaving or have you realised yet that he can be a bit of a numpty sometimes?" she laughed. Pam didn't laugh. She just smiled affectionately.

Tabitha suddenly realised that these two really were getting serious and maybe she should in fact be a little more respectful of her friend's boyfriend, even if he was her big brother. Her mind began to wander. Which side of the church would she sit on if they got married? What would she wear? Would she be part of the wedding party?

Laura put her glass down carefully and looked at Tabitha with a serious expression. "Well actually Tabitha, there is something that I wanted to speak with you about."

"Ooh that sounds ominous", Tabitha replied, looking at Pam to see if she knew what was going on.

Pam looked like she was in the know but she avoided Tabitha's glance and examined her nails studiously.

"Well see, the thing is", Laura said slowly. "I've been feeling a bit overwhelmed with the kids and stuff."

Tabitha was instantly concerned about her friend and gently touched her arm in support.

"Oh, it's fine hon. Nothing out of the ordinary, according to Mums.net, but well, now that they're getting a bit older, Martin has suggested that I find something to do that's just for me. You know, like a hobby and I wondered if you fancy doing something with me?"

Tabitha released her concerned breath. " Of course hon, I'd love to. Whatever you fancy." It sounded like a great idea to Tabitha. She could definitely benefit too from a hobby outside of work and it would be great to spend more time with Laura and maybe even discover herself more with a new skill. Maybe yoga or a cookery class.

Laura clapped her hands together excitedly as Pam nodded, wide eyed and grinning, beside her. Tabitha noted, with trepidation, that her best friend was managing to look even more shifty by the second.

"So, I saw a poster for a ladies football team. How fun would that be?" Laura beamed at Tabitha, awaiting a delighted response.

Tabitha however, felt as though she had just been winded by a football and she searched desperately for the right words to let her friend down gently.

"Ah, um, I'm so sorry Laura but let me introduce myself. I'm your friend Tabitha and I'm godawful at all sports. Don't you remember in rounders at school when we'd get out immediately and spend most of the lesson watching everybody else?"

"Yeah of course Tabs but that's cos we wanted to get run out so we could sit and sunbathe. This would be different because we'd want to do well."

Tabitha scratched the back of her scalp, feeling like there was an immediate patch of stress induced eczema on it's way.

"And you go running Tabitha", Laura continued. "You're fitter than most people I know."

"I do run, that's true", Tabitha replied, before taking a large gulp of her drink.

"Well I suppose we could go along and see what they say. If I don't make the team maybe I could be a mascot or do they have cheerleaders?"

"That's my girl. You will make the team. It's gonna be fab". Laura was bouncing in her chair now. "I'm gonna send you some video clips of basic skills and I brought you this."

With that, Laura reached under the table and pulled out a football and handed it to Tabitha.

"Ok coach", laughed Tabitha. "So I guess that me saying no wasn't an option. How long do I have?"

Pam giggled as she drank, causing bubbles to rise in her glass.

"The next kickabout for interested newbies is on Thursday", confessed Laura, looking guilty but amused.

Pam laughed loudly now as Tabitha swallowed hard.

"Um excuse me", Tabitha shook her head as the realisation hit her, "How come you aren't getting involved dear girl?"

Pam patted her on the back consolingly. "Oh honey, I really was first out in rounders because I was rubbish. You know I don't actually like sunbathing. More drinks ladies?"

Tabitha laughed as her friend bolted to the safety of the bar. At least Pam was making herself useful, she supposed. Tabitha quickly concluded that if she was going to be a professional sportswoman she had better make the most of being allowed to drink for the time being.

CHAPTER
SEVENTEEN

Well they say that time flies when you're having fun. What they don't make such a big deal of is how time flies when you are due to do something that you are dreading and you already have hardly any time to prepare for it.

Four days later, Tabitha looked around at the rest of the group gathered on the pitch at the sports club. There was a mixture of facial expressions, some very excited and others that shared her own slightly nervous and dazed expression, presumably other friends that had been persuaded to come along like herself.

Tabitha jogged on the spot, aware that this might give off the wrong impression that she was a bit of a jock, whereas really she was just trying to warm up a little. She could see her breath in the cold air and it wasn't something that she was a fan of. She prayed once more that she wouldn't be way out of her league and then inwardly congratulated herself on the accidental pun.

Suddenly there was a hush as everybody looked round at the two ladies who had emerged from the clubhouse and were headed towards them. One, immediately reminded Tabitha of an old gym teacher from school. She had the strong, confident appearance of somebody who could have made the Olympics for most sports, had she chosen to, but hadn't followed that path and would eternally punish others for it with various drills involving bean bags and plastic skittles.

The shorter lady beside her carried a clipboard and had a pencil protruding precariously from her hair. She looked as if maybe she could be doing this for fun in her retirement and she gave a warm smile to the girls.

Tabitha couldn't believe how nervous she felt right now. She had been meeting all kinds of important people at Yerans and yet here, at an event that was supposed to be fun, she felt like she was an imposter.

The Gym teacher lady surveyed the group before her. "Ok you lot, in a row please. Let's have a look at ya", she boomed.

Even the comfortable people looked a little apprehensive now and Tabitha found herself nervously pulling her shorts out of her bottom. Everybody scurried to form a neat row.

"This is like the beginning of an Officer and a Gentleman, I'm scared", Tabitha whispered to Laura.

Gym teacher lady glared over at them. She spoke to her colleague whilst nodding towards Tabitha and Laura and her dutiful comrade scribbled down a note.

"Right then ladies", she boomed. "I do hope you're all ready to show me what you've got."

"Yes ma'am", the group mumbled, not really knowing what to call her and eventually copying each other's response.

"Good. My name is Jillian and this is Val. My friends call me Jill....You can't."

'Holy cow', thought Tabitha. 'What on earth have we got ourselves into.' The only Jillian that she could think of was the toughnut trainer on The Biggest loser who had always given her Sarah Connor vibes. She snuck a peek at Laura who was also looking quite uncertain now. Poor

Laura. Her plan to come along here had been intended to provide some chill out time.

"Ok, I want you to split into four groups, you, you, you there, you there, you and you..."

As she directed everybody into their places, Tabitha just knew that she was going to be split up from Laura. She shouldn't have gotten caught whispering. God, this was just like school all over again. True enough, they were stripped from the security blanket of each other. She smiled at the two other girls she had been teamed up with.

"Right, you guys, I want to see your burpees, you three press ups, you lot star jumps and"...Tabitha was horrified. This wasn't even football. This was aerobics and with all her least favourite exercises too... "and you three can run over there and grab those balls please." With that she blew shrilly on her whistle.

Tabitha decided that now was certainly not a time to giggle at the phrase that would usually have been rewarded with a cheeky chuckle. Well, at least there was going to be some football involved. Tabitha was relieved, as she had actually followed Laura's instructions and had eventually come to some sort of a relationship between her foot and a football, despite it being a very casual thing.

The next forty five minutes were exhausting. Tabitha wiped sweat from her brow after doing what felt like her three hundredth press up. She wished that she hadn't had to resign to doing press ups on her knees as they were frozen through now.

It had transpired that the three rounds of exercises continued for the entire session except for when in the one group that was working with Jillian on ball drills. As Tabitha noticed a streak of sweaty mud on her hand, she wondered if she had just rubbed mud onto or from her forehead. She asked herself if this was for her at all. It was really messy and hard.

Jillian finally blew her whistle to summon the group back together and began to confer with Val, studying the notes that had been scribbled down. Tabitha was grateful to get her breath back and was now appreciative of the cold air.

As the girls stood and waited for their evaluation, weirdly now that it was all over, Tabitha began to experience a curious feeling of gleeful achievement. She wondered what on earth was wrong with her and decided that she must either be some kind of masochist or that her endorphins were tricking her. She'd not fainted with exhaustion though and actually felt that she'd exceeded her own expectations. Maybe it was a shame that she wouldn't make the team after all. It might have gotten easier eventually she guessed.

"Ok ladies, back in line for me please, chop chop", Jillian commanded.

Everybody moved a little slower this time to form an orderly line in front of their newly acquired master. The ladies all looked around at each other, eyeing up the competition and wondering who might have made it into the squad.

Gym teacher Jillian suddenly burst into a massive grin and clapped her hands.

"Well girls, you were all great", she exclaimed cheerily. "Your most important football lessons were learnt today. You were tough in adversity, disciplined and best of all, supportive to each other. I'll see you all next week."

There were murmurs of surprise around the group.

"Any questions?" asked Val, sounding like she kind of hoped that there wouldn't be.

A few hands went up reluctantly, nobody wanting to be the first one.

"Yes dear". Val pointed to a young athletic girl who had already looked like an established footballer.

"Um, when do we meet the rest of the squad and how many are there? I mean if there are 12 of us here..?"

Val looked to Jillian to see if she wanted to answer but Jillian deliberately averted her glance. Val shook her head as if she felt a little dropped in it.

"Ok girls, here's the thing. You kind of are the team."

Everybody gasped together..as a team.

"Well actually, not completely, there are six girls left from the original team but um.."

She looked again at Jillian who pretended not to see as she gazed up at a plane going over.

"We've found ourselves in a bit of a pickle. You see, the girls here used to get a few small perks, kit provided, lunch on match days but well, times are a little tough. We've dropped low in the league, leading to our sponsors bailing on us and every penny we can raise on a match day now is going on travel and hiring places for training."

Jillian sniffed and looked away from the shocked stares. It seemed now that she wasn't anywhere near as tough as she had been pretending to be and that little Val, in fact, was the one holding things together here right now. She touched Jillian's arm comfortingly as she continued.

"Anyway our best players decided that they wanted to jump ship to a rival club nearby, who have lots of nice things and a good chance of promotion to the area's top league." She shook her head. "They've got so many damn players now that some of our girls aren't even getting to play at all, but there we are." Val sniffed now and it was Jillian's turn to help out her friend.

"So, yes ladies", Jillian concluded. "If you want it, you are the team. It might not last for long I'm afraid though. Unless we can avoid relegation and attract a new sponsor, I'm not sure how we can continue next season but we can give this a crack hey? At least get this season finished off?"

She looked around at the 'team' who all seemed too startled to speak now.

"Any more questions ladies", Val invited, looking really hopeful now that there wouldn't be.

Nobody moved. There didn't seem to be much more to ask right now.

"Right then", Jillian boomed, finding her strong voice once more. "We'll hope to see you all here at the same time, next week. There'll be no more nasty aerobics, it'll be football all the way....as we have a match two days after that. Oh by the way, anybody that comes back can call me Jill."

CHAPTER EIGHTEEN

"So you're an actual footballer now then? Are we allowed to come and watch you play?

Peter had darted to Tabitha's desk, the moment she arrived in the office, closely followed by Kelly.

"What, how do you even know?" enquired Tabitha, gobsmacked. She turned to Marnie who just looked plain guilty.

Marnie had no option but to confess her involvement in the newscast. "Well, I bumped into Daniel in the canteen whose sister is friends with Fran, your friend Laura's cousin.

Tabitha blinked, trying to follow the trail. "Wow I guess it's a slow news day if we're the hot topic", she laughed.

"Well, you know, on my part and in my defence, ooh defence, that's like a football thing init?" Marnie cracked up at herself and received a high five from Kelly. "Sorry

Tabs, It's just that I don't really know Daniel that well so I guess he was looking to talk about people we had in common. I'm not sure how it had already got quite that far so quickly but you are big news my lovely". Marnie shrugged now as if it wasn't actually that much to do with her at all, despite the fact that she'd obviously already carried on the information trail to both Kelly and Peter, at least.

Tabitha laughed. "Well I wouldn't exactly say that I'm a footballer anyway. I'm aching like mad and I think I might have broken a toe."

Her friends pulled sympathetic faces briefly before Peter repeated impatiently, "So are we allowed to come and watch you play?"

"Not yet", Tabitha grimaced. "I already nearly got in trouble for being disruptive. I don't need you hooligans around. And I need to get better first.....if I can."

Lizzie came out of her office then and headed towards the stairs. She stopped in her tracks as she saw the group of friends huddled together and rushed over.

"Oops", said Kelly. "Busted dossing again. She gets me everytime."

Lizzie beamed though as she joined them and pointed finger guns at Tabitha in apparent approval of her, not at all secret new hobby whilst hilariously singing the Ski sunday song.

Tabitha was gratefully saved from all of the madness by her phone ringing and her friends reluctantly went on their way.

That evening, Tabitha peered out of the bus window on her way home. The Christmas lights had been erected in town, though not yet lit. The illumination would take place next week at the push of a button by an up and coming superstar singer that Tabitha had never heard of. Was she really that old already that she was losing touch with what was cool? Well nevermind, she thought, I'm gonna be a footballer, a girl footballer. She decided that that was pretty cool. It didn't matter if she didn't know about every single person on the celebrity pages if she was doing something awesome herself.

Except, she wasn't a footballer. She was just a girl that had gone along to a football training session and had somehow found herself in a football team. What if it all went wrong when they played a game? What if she air kicked at an open goal? Oh well, she knew the terms air kick and open goal so that was a start but crikey, she had one more practise before their match. There was only one thing for it. She'd have to tell her brother what was going on and ask for his help.

She remembered that he had been a good player when he was at college. In fact he probably started to get pretty good from about the age of ten because that was when she didn't get to play with him and his friends so much anymore. She'd sit on the swings and watch them instead. She would see him look over every now and again to make sure she was ok and she always felt special. Some of her friends' older siblings wouldn't let them even be seen with them. As much as George would muck about and tease her, he always had her back. Let's hope that he could save her now.

She sent him a message with a quick summary of the predicament that she had found herself in and requested his assistance any evening in the next week that suited him.

Her phone pinged straight away.

Ha ha, Pam said you'd got proper stitched up! Nice one! No worries Sis. I'll see you at the park tomorrow, 5:30....PM that is!!! x

Tabitha let out a sigh of relief as she took comfort in the fact that there was nothing else that she could do about the issue right now. She'd put it away until tomorrow. Or actually, her mind fought back, maybe she should put together an eating plan for the next day to help with stamina. Yes, she'd google what athletes ate once she got home. Eggs must be a good option for breakfast, she decided, but she'd need to set her alarm a bit earlier. Maybe she could have her shower tonight. Oh, and she could have all her clothes ready to change into after she finished work then that would help her to relax throughout the day so she could forget about everything until she got to the park.

Tabitha was suddenly amused that she was already building all her plans around something that she had only heard about less than a week ago. She wasn't surprised though. As usual she was finding that she was an all or nothing girl and it appeared that this new venture was going to be given her all too. She looked back out of the window with a grin, feeling much less daunted now that she had everything arranged in her head, until she realised that she was four or five stops past her house. And so training started early with a gentle jog home in her work shoes.

CHAPTER NINETEEN

As Tabitha headed over to her brother's van the next evening, she was surprised to see Scott's car parked up alongside him. They both climbed out of the van and folded their arms as she approached them, looking like they meant serious business.

'Well football's not fun anymore', thought Tabitha.

"Alright our kid", George took in Tabitha's trainers as he spoke. "Hmm, ok we have a lot of work to do. For a start, those shoes might be fine for track running or hanging about outside the cinema with your buddies but you're gonna need something a bit more sturdy for footie."

Tabitha laughed. She hadn't hung around outside the cinema for about ten years but bless him.

"Ok your training starts here. Listen well youngling."

It's two years, Tabitha thought to herself. I'm two years younger. Youngling, my butt. Then she reprimanded herself. Now was not the time. George was here to help her.

"Right, the problem with football these days is that so many teams are over coached. It's all 'draw the man before you pass blah blah blah' but if you drawing your man means that the player you're passing to is now being covered better, then it's a bad move right?"

"Right...so.... I don't draw the man?" Tabitha enquired.

"Well sometimes you do, sometimes you don't. What you do do".

Tabitha laughed, George frowned.

"Sorry but you said do do".

George shook his head. "What I would like. you. to. do is to make your own decisions on the pitch, react to the game that's in front of you. When you're at a Reading game, you're watching and thinking what should happen next, switch the ball over to the left cos there's space there, long ball to that guy making a run. Well this is the same as that, except that you're actually the player. You don't get as good a view of the pitch I'm afraid as when you're in the stands or watching on the telly, but take the time to look up, see where your players are, who's free, who's moving."

"Right, cool", Tabitha agreed, impressed at her brother's coaching skills even though they did involve telling her not to be over coached.

"Ok this session is going to be all about what wins a game of football for you and your team and that is...?

He paused and held out his hand to Tabitha, inviting the answer.

"Um fitness?"

George shook his head.

"Skills? Tenacity, Spirit and Flare?" she laughed.

"Goals Tabitha, Goals. The only thing that gets you the points when the final whistle blows is having scored more goals than the other team."

Vindaloo immediately popped into Tabitha's head. She was about to start singing 'na na na' but George was looking very serious.

"Yeah I know", he laughed, also picking up on what he'd said, "na na na, na na na, but right now, no no no. There will be times when playing football will be joyous and fun but not yet. Now we work. So Scott is here to play in goal for us."

Scott grinned at Tabitha then raised his hand obediently, looking like he didn't want to risk getting into trouble with their new apparent gaffer.

"I will be crossing the ball from various places and you will be kicking the ball past Scott into the goal. Simples."

"Cool", Tabitha agreed, praying that she'd at least get some shots on target.

Her first shot was the highly anticipated and much dreaded air kick and Tabitha hung her head in frustration.

"Never hang your head", shouted George. "If you make a howler and need to react, you look to the sky, not the floor alright. Head up."

"Um ok", Tabitha agreed, feeling that those words definitely fitted into the overcoaching category..

"Ok Tabby. Again."

As George's crosses kept being delivered, Tabitha began to connect with the ball better, sometimes controlling it before shooting and sometimes hitting it whilst it was still moving. More and more were on target for the goal and finally she managed to get a few past Scott.

As it began to get dark, rain started to drizzle down on them. Tabitha was hungry now so she wasn't too disappointed that they would have to call it a day.

George wandered over. "Right, you still alright for time Scott?"

"Yeah man, I'm good mate."

"Nice one. Ok Tabitha. We're gonna try out your left foot now."

Tabitha looked up at the rain and the clouds that were beginning to move across the sky quite dramatically.

"Now now Sis. What are you gonna do if you're playing a match and it starts raining, run indoors to stop your hair going curly? Now get back out there."

Tabitha saluted. "Yes boss." She walked back towards the goal, holding her lower back as she went, thinking of a nice warm bath.

George called out after her. "Not much longer alright. You're doing really good. Now let's see about this left foot.

After another twenty minutes, the three of them were having a great time. After all, once you're soaked through, you can't get any wetter so may as well just embrace it. Somehow, despite being right handed and instinctively kicking the ball with her right foot, Tabitha's left foot was a lightning bolt. Ball after ball fired towards the goal.

Eventually she began to correctly anticipate which way Scott would move and aimed the ball at the opposite corner. She felt proud of herself as she realised that he was no longer giving her any easy chances to help her confidence as he sprung high in the air and dove to the floor, sliding along the mud to keep out some of her shots.

The rain got heavier and the wind stronger but Tabitha didn't care anymore. The adrenaline was surging through her. She could do this. How bloody awesome.

It was now her that was slightly disappointed when George picked up the ball and walked over.

"Ok that should set you up alright for your first game at least. Now let's get out of here. Mum will kill me if you get ill and can't play at all."

The three of them scurried back to the car park. Tabitha couldn't believe what they had achieved since she had walked across the park two hours ago.

Once they were back in the lit up area, Tabitha was shocked at how much mud they had managed to acquire in such a short time. Fairplay to George's opinion on her trainers. They would need a good clean if they were to be rescued at all and she would need to get something more suitable before the match. Her hands and knees were caked in mud. 'What a look', she thought. Nobody could say that she hadn't given her all to embracing this challenge. Surely even Jillian would have been impressed.

"Well excuse me guys but I've just had my car cleaned", Scott apologised as he pulled his sweatshirt over his head and popped it in his boot.

Tabitha would later blame it on tiredness, hunger, maybe even the fact that they had just trained together and they were now close teammates but her eyes became shamelessly transfixed on his body. She'd never seen him topless before. I mean why would she have? But now she had, and well..wow.

"See you later Morris's. Thanks for letting me join yous. That was a blast", the new hunky Scott called over.

"Cheers mate", George shouted over the wind as Scott walked round to his driving seat. "I appreciate you helping out."

George looked at Tabitha, wondering where his sister's manners had got to as she failed to thank Scott.

Tabitha was still just staring at Scott with her head slightly tilted. George gave her a nudge, bringing her back to the reality of her appalling behaviour.

"Oh, yeah, thanks so much Scott. I hope I'll do you proud. Safe journey. See you about", she babbled inanely.

Scott waved and drove off.

"What the dickens was that?" George looked beyond baffled.

"What? I don't know what you..".

"You, you big perv, letching at Scott."

"Hey dude, I wasn't letching." Tabitha declared, far too shrilly to sound convincing. She was far from convinced herself, Had she been letching? How uncivilised…and right in front of her brother. Ew how embarrassing.

"Oh I get it. Are you messing with me cos I'm seeing Pam? I thought you were ok about that."

"I'm not.. I mean I am ok about you and Pam..I love you and Pam together. I meant I'm not messing with you, I was just deep in thought and Scott was in my eyeline.

"So what on earth were you thinking about?"

Tabitha looked around, desperate for inspiration.

"Um…" She shouted the first thing that caught her eye. "Scott's ball!", she offered, thinking that would clear things up.

George covered his ears and winced. "Oh god, just get in the van. I'll drop you home. I've got a date with a tax form that's more appealing than this conversation."

"Oh no bro, I mean Scott forgot to take his ball home. Jeez". Tabitha stifled a laugh as she realised what she had said, deciding that silence was probably now her best option.

George seemed traumatised enough and any talking she did now would be lying anyway as she couldn't get away from the fact that she had just simply been staring at Scott and thinking about what a beautiful body he had. Oh bugger. That was weird.

When she got home, Snuggles came running out to greet her, took one look and turned around again. Tabitha hoped that it was the sight of the mud splattered up her legs and not the smell of shame that had disgusted her little housemate.

As she closed her eyes in bed that night, the image of Scott raising his shirt over his head kept repeating. The clip ran in slow motion, rain trickling over his torso, those lucky drops caressing his tight body. What the? She told herself to stop thinking about him. It was Scott for goodness sake. She'd known him forever. He would be horrified.

She tried to think of something else. Somebody else. What about Billy the kid? Yes, think about him. Think about Billy in the pool....Nope, that wasn't gonna work. They had spoken on the phone a couple of times and it was definitely just a friend thing.

It was still Scott! This was not good. Desperate times called for desperate measures and she tried to block out the pictures of Scott by making herself think about Gary.

Nope, definitely nothing there anymore. Well that was good she surmised but darn. Tabitha bit her lip as an imaginary raindrop teased all the way down to Scott's waist.

She was just going to have to sleep on it. It'd be gone by tomorrow. It'd all be fine. She was just overtired. Then came the dream.

CHAPTER TWENTY

"Darling, I'm starting to think that you're avoiding my cooking. This is the third time you've turned down dinner. Are you sure you're ok?"

"Yeah I'm sure Mum. It's just been a really busy day. You know we have to be ready to film in Paris in a couple of weeks. I've been at the Yerans offices all day and I have football training after work tomorrow. I just really need to get my stuff together tonight"

"Oh yes. The footie. Is that why you're not coming round for my goulash? Are you like a proper athlete now? Body is a temple and all that jazz?"

Tabitha laughed. "Hardly Mum, we lost 5-1 last weekend."

"But you did score the one though darling. I was so proud when you text. I can't believe you won't let us all come to see you play yet."

"Mum, we conceded five..and anyway it was freezing. You wouldn't have enjoyed yourself."

"Well maybe I'll get to come along soon and I'll just bring a nice hot toddy in a flask."

"Oh crikey, so you're gonna be the tipsy soccer Mom of a 25 year old. Jesus wept!"

"Oh dear, darling, there's no need for blasphemy. Anyway, the boys have just pulled up. They'll be excited to get extra goulash. Three Hail Marys for you for the blasphemy and please make sure you eat something decent. I'll be texting to check later."

"Sure, bye Mum. Love you."

"Love you sweetheart. I'll send your best to the boys."

Tabitha tossed her phone onto the cushion beside her and returned her attention to her family bag of toffee popcorn.

"The boys, Snuggles. Mum will send my best to the boys. My best what…apologies, blushes. Oh dear dear. What an awful jam I've got myself in."

Tabitha hadn't been lying about being busy, but she wasn't actually busy enough to have avoided 'the boys' for a whole two weeks and two days now.

But well, the dream had happened. There was no way that she could face Scott at the moment. She was certain that he'd know. Either she was going to see him and visibly swoon or she would look at him and he would just be good old Scott again and she was sure then that he'd see the disappointment in her face. The poor guy couldn't win. And yet he hadn't even done anything wrong, well actually he had. He'd removed his top and flaunted himself at her, her in her vulnerable state of accidental celibacy.

She'd actually come clean to Pam eventually but only because, after three gin and tonics one night, she had become loose lipped. Pam had wanted every detail of the dream and her chin was nearly on the table as Tabitha told her just half of what had happened. Pam had sworn blind not to say anything to George but well, they were a couple now. Tabitha couldn't be 100% certain that her brother wasn't aware and quite rightly ashamed of her.

Well she'd have to find out soon. It was Christmas day next week and it would have been beyond peculiar if she had turned down that meal at her Mum's. She was just going to have to face the music.

There was one football match scheduled before Christmas then just one more before Paris. The team was going to have to be without her when she went away then they would play the final game of the season on her return. It was looking like it would be their final game altogether.

They had played two, lost two since the team had been put together. Weirdly though they'd still had a great time. Practices had become more fun and, to be fair, Laura had only suggested going along to the football for a bit of a laugh in the first place.

As the nights had got increasingly colder, Tabitha had appreciated being pushed harder and faster in training and she felt good for it. She was so much stronger than she realised and was actually not an awful footballer either. She was so grateful for the breakthrough that she'd experienced due to her brother's perseverance.

She felt bad that she would miss the penultimate match but delighted, of course, that she had been invited to Paris. Three adverts were being filmed there due to it being in close proximity to three of their chosen stars, a huge film star, a rugby player and also a musician whose show would be touring through there at the same time.

Yerans decided that obviously it made much more sense to go to them rather than wait for all three of the advert's stars to be available in the uk. Tabitha had agreed wholeheartedly with their decision before even realising that she was being invited along to watch one of the adverts being filmed.

What better way to carry on the excitement of the Christmas season than a little trip to Paris. Seeing in the New year in another country might be a little strange but novel all the same.

Unfortunately, Jillian and Val weren't quite so excited when she told them. She had made sure to arrive early to training so that she could speak to them before the rest of the team arrived. She felt horrible enough. She didn't need an audience.

Jillian asked immediately if the trip could be postponed until after the season had finished.

Val looked at her aghast. "Jillian dear, have you heard of Yerans?"

"Well yes, of course I have. I actually have one of their products in my glovebox right now."

"Right. Surely then you realise that they are a little bit bigger than our wee team here. Tabitha has a life outside of football and this is a fantastic opportunity for her so stop guilting her ok?"

"Yes boss", laughed Jillian.

Tabitha allowed herself to break a smile, despite her dismay at letting these two adorable ladies down. So apparently Val was top dog around here after all, despite the good cop, bad cop act given by them on the first training day. She needed to bear that in mind. You obviously didn't need to go stamping about to attain power and respect from one's peers.

"I'm just scared, you know", Jillian shrugged her shoulders, "The game that Tabitha is missing is kind of our last chance for points in my books. I don't think we can even dream of getting anything against Sonning in the final match."

Tabitha gasped. "Oh no. Sonning are our final match? You mean where all your girls went? I mean haven't they only been beaten twice this season? And that was before they stole half of Woodley's team? Shiiiii."

"Tabitha!" Val interjected. "I shan't have that language or that doubt from any of my girls. This is not over till I say so, ok?" Tabitha nodded. "Now I'd rather not talk about this yet, Jill. If the girls haven't noticed that we have Sonning on the fixture list then I think that's for the best. It's the main reason I'm saying to focus on one match at a time. We need to keep spirits high ok?"

Just then a few of the team began to arrive. Tabitha responded accordingly to a subtle nod from Val and threw her head back and laughed at an imaginary joke. Jillian joined in appropriately and training for what now felt to be the last three matches, not four began in earnest.

CHAPTER TWENTY ONE

"And then Samantha struck it down the left wing and I got it and I crossed it into the box like we'd practised and Tabitha just goddamn thwacked it into the goal. Their goalie hardly even had time to see it go past her. It was soooo awesome. I can't believe we actually won a game."

"That does sound awesome Laura to be fair and you know I'm not really into sports." Pam blew a bubble with her bubblegum and popped it skillfully with her finger.

Laura's kids gasped in awe then turned their attention back to their iced snowflake cookies.

"So, when can we come and see you guys play for goodness sake?" Pam asked. "Your poor brother is quite gutted he hasn't been invited, although he'd never say of course."

Tabitha sighed. It was going to be such extra pressure but if it was all gonna be over soon, she was going to have to give in and let them come along.

"Well I guess next weekend will be ok. I expect there will be quite a few people coming along as it's between Christmas and New year."

"Yay, that's settled then girls. I'll bring my pom poms and get a chant sorted."

"Oh no, please don't hon", laughed Tabitha. "I'll be in pieces. Anyways, I really need to get a shimmy on if anybody is getting any Christmas presies from me this year. Have a great Christmas Laura and you two precious ones. Pamela, weirdly I'll see you at my Mum's."

The girls exchanged hugs and Tabitha headed out into the chilly afternoon, throwing her scarf across her face to protect herself from the windchill. The Christmas decorations looked stunning, even with some daylight left. Blue and white icicles cascaded down the sides of the tall buildings and huge illuminated stars twinkled along the middle of the walkway.

Tabitha was relieved that she had put together a bit of a purchase plan as it appeared that she certainly wasn't the only person who had left their shopping until the last weekend before Christmas. She had planned to shop earlier but life had become so full these days.

She peered along the street to make sure that Next was still where it had been the last time she'd shopped. Things changed so quickly on the high street. Christmas shopping was certainly more challenging now that BHS and Woolworths were no longer about.

Tabitha had heard a few years back that there was still a BHS in Gibraltar long after it had left Britain's streets but she had decided that it would be a bit extreme to travel that far just to check out if it was as she remembered.

The air was filled with the smells of roasted chestnuts and cinnamon from the Christmas stalls. Tabitha smiled over at the excited children, queueing to purchase their personalised stockings, all ready for Santa.

Just then she heard a booming laugh beside her that she recognised from somewhere and then she collided with it.

"I'm so sorry", the familiar voice declared. "Oh gosh, Hi Tabitha darlin'".

"Hi Steve, it's been ages. How are you?"

"I'm doing great. Hey, weren't we crashing into people the last time I saw you? Mind, we were Scottish country dancing and a little drunk then." Steve flinched at his own words as he recalled that that day hadn't transpired to end too well for Tabitha. "Um, I was just laughing at that poor gal trying to keep her hat on."

Tabitha followed his gaze to a lady, laden with shopping bags and wearing a huge wide brimmed hat with the price tag still attached.

She was sure that she had seen her friend somewhere before but couldn't place her at first. Then she remembered. She had been at the rock show. It was her boyfriend that had been playing the drums that night and had declared his love for her in front of everybody. Sarah? Yes that was it, Sarah. The stranger who had inspired her to know how she wanted to be loved in the future. She smiled at the memory and turned her attention back to Steve.

"How have you been, Tabitha? I mean, I guess a lot has changed since I saw you last". Steve went a little red in the face and it occurred to Tabitha that he probably didn't know that she was aware of everything that had changed since she'd been out of touch with them all.

"I'm really good, thanks Steve. I wasn't for a short while but now I know I'm better off where I am now. And you look really well."

"Well, I've actually been seeing this girl that turned my life around. I'm totally clean now. The only high I get is from the gym."

Steve looked down at his feet and shuffled them about awkwardly.

"That's brilliant. Good for you. Is it Vanessa by any chance?" Tabitha felt slightly queasy as she said her name out loud but couldn't bear the tension any longer.

"Uh yeah, how do you..?"

"Gary", laughed Tabitha whilst shaking her head. "The turd came to me for comfort when it happened."

"Oh damn, I'm really sorry about that Tabitha. That's kind of sick..and not the cool meaning of sick right?"

"Yeah it was a bit messed up but it was the final thing I needed, to really know that I was better off without him. How is he? Are you guys ok now?"

Steve rubbed his temple. "Not completely. We talk a little because of work so that's a start. He got a transfer and seems ok. I guess maybe one day…"

"Hey babe, What about this one? Oh..shit…hi."

Vanessa suddenly appeared in the doorway holding up a babygrow.

The three of them stood in a triangle waiting for each other to speak. It reminded Tabitha of the Good, the bad and the ugly. As the music from the film popped into her head she had an appreciated flashback of sweet Billy. She looked at Steve then at Vanessa. Who was who from the film, she wondered? Well, she decided, she didn't deserve to be the bad and didn't fancy being the ugly so she was just gonna have to be the Good.

She took a deep breath and smiled. "Hi Vanessa." She looked back at Steve. "Well you guys didn't waste any time. I think that one is a perfect choice."

Steve looked confused for a minute then realised that Tabitha was talking about the babygrow. "Oh crikey", he laughed. "Nah that's for my brother's little poop machine. I'm handing over the responsibility of choosing something as Vanessa is such a fan of kids."

He winked at Tabitha as he said it.

"Yeah ok hon", huffed Vanessa, "I can't stand kids but I knew I'd be quicker so we can get the hell out of here."

"Yeah, it is kinda busy", Tabitha answered cordially.

Silence transcended again.

"Anyway, it was nic...", Tabitha tried to save them all from the embarrassing situation.

"Look Tabitha", Vanessa interrupted. "I'm really sorry about what happened with Gary. He'd played down your relationship. By the time I met you..well...look I'm just sorry that you got hurt."

"Thanks Vanessa. I appreciate your apology. Look, it is what it is."

Steve looked like he would rather be anywhere else right now.

"Anyway, I've got to get on guys but defo buy that babygrow. It's gorgeous and well..have a good Christmas hey."

"You too Tabitha", Steve smiled warmly. "It was really good to see you."

Tabitha waved and in her flustered state, headed back the same way that she had just come, aware that her purchase plan had now gone to pot.

She tried to assess how she felt; shocked as the meeting had come out of the blue, relieved that the air had been cleared but a little angry too. Vanessa may have been all sweetness and light with her apology but she was certainly no goddamn angel. She had cheated on Gary with Steve after all, his friend for goodness sake, as well as the incident of kissing Gary when he was her boyfriend.

And even if he had played down the relationship, she had still known that there was a relationship.

Anyway, in conclusion of it all, Vanessa had Steve on the straight and narrow now and that was great news. It sounded like Gary was doing ok and the best thing of all was that Tabitha's life was full and happy away from all their drama.

She found a bench near to a group of carol singers where she could reassess her presie plan and she ended up just sitting and listening for the next twenty minutes, smiling at the cheerful families pausing on their way past.

It was good to just take a moment. Life was good. Exciting things were happening and she felt at peace.

CHAPTER TWENTY TWO

Christmas day turned out to be one of the strangest that Tabitha had ever known. Two days before Christmas, her Mum had messaged her and George to inform them that their Father would now be joining them for Christmas lunch. Apparently he'd had another barney with Fiona and that was definitely the end this time.

Tabitha's parents had remained great friends since their divorce, so much so that they had all been at Dad and Fiona's wedding together four years ago.

Christmas dinner with her Mother and Father was going to be weird though. That was a whole other level. Tabitha was disappointed that her Dad and Fiona had fallen out. They were a great match but they drove each other crazy over the silliest of things. They literally could row over the remote control. Tabitha sometimes wondered if they simply enjoyed the drama and the joy of getting back together again.

On Christmas eve Tabitha received a call from her Mum informing her that the lovebirds had now reunited. Tabitha was a little disappointed that her Father wouldn't be joining them after all, now that she had managed to get her head round it.

"Oh no, he's coming love", Mum had explained. "So is Fiona and so is Archie. I've just sent your brother off for more food although they must have got stuff in at theirs....anyway. Poor George only popped round to drop presents off and have a quick cuppa and I've ordered him off down to Sainsburys with a list as long as his arm. I mean really, it's just like your Father to drop that on me at the last minute, he's always been a liability but he's not supposed to still be my liability, for crying out loud."

Tabitha smirked. She knew that Mum was proper fond of him really. So it really was going to be a full house at Mum's. Archie was Fiona's son who had just become an official teenager, despite practising for quite a while now, according to Fiona so Tabitha assumed that he would rather be gaming than hanging out with his step dad's old family on Christmas day. The poor thing.

She was proved very wrong though. However Archie was behaving at home these days, he was an absolute pleasure to spend Christmas with. He was polite and entertaining at the table, sharing stories from school.

The grown ups all laughed together, Mum and Fiona ganged up on Tabitha's Dad which they all enjoyed and George and Pam just grinned at each other and everybody and everything all afternoon. Tabitha could almost see a big pink love heart glowing around the two of them.

Tabitha surveyed their throw together family and felt warm inside. If this wasn't what Christmas was all about then who knew what was.

After dinner, her Father fell asleep in front of Only fools and horses, despite Mum and Fiona singing along to Wham on the radio as they cleared up the kitchen. Their volume gradually increased as they supped the brandy left over from the Christmas pudding pyrotechnic display but Father's traditional nap withstood the challenge.

Tabitha offered to help out with the washing up but Mum flicked her tea towel at her dismissively and summoned George over.

"You've still got a presie from your brother to open Tabby. You kids all run along outside and get some fresh air. You too Archie. You'll like it. We'll be fine". With that her Mum topped up their drinks a little. "Won't we Fi? '", she chuckled as they clinked their glasses together.

Tabitha couldn't think what her present could be that needed to be outside. She'd always wanted a pony but wasn't sure that there had been one hiding out in Mum's back garden all day. George and Pam hurried her out of the door excitedly.

As she walked along the garden she discovered a goal shaped present which could actually only be a goal. "Oh my goodness, how did you get Mum to agree to this, her poor grass", laughed Tabitha.

"Well Sis, I explained that as today was a Thursday, you'd be missing a training session. As you guys have only got a few more matches, it's our duty to make sure that you practise."

"It's awesome George. Thank you so much."

"No probs Sis. We're really proud of you. Now let's get some work done hey kid?"

Tabitha beamed. She couldn't even be cross with her brother for calling her kid when he'd just declared his pride for her. How perfect was this day, Tabitha thought. For the next hour the four of them ran around and laughed together. Even Pam looked like she was actually enjoying playing a sport.

They only stopped when Tabitha's Mum called them in. "The Snowman is about to start kids. Let's all watch it together huh?"

George ruffled Archie's hair as they headed up the garden and Tabitha linked arms with Pam. As they all wandered inside for Christmas tv and more food, the snow began to fall.

Tabitha headed to bed that night, full of love and the chocolate money that Santa had put under Mum's tree for her. Santa's handwriting was uncannily like her Mother's. She took one last look out of her bedroom window at the snow that had settled in her garden. What a perfect end to a very special day. Maybe tomorrow she would even build a snowman if the snow stayed.

CHAPTER TWENTY THREE

After a chilled Boxing day where Tabitha did get to build a bit of a wonky snowman in between eating, working out and then eating again, match day arrived.

She had made a food plan for the morning. With a 1pm kick off she knew that she needed to eat well but not too close to playing. She didn't really feel that much like eating this early in the day after the last two days of overindulging. She was nervous too. It was such a big match. It was almost imperative that they got a win today.

Tabitha scrolled through facebook as she poked at her porridge, excited to see everybody's Christmas photos. Suddenly her phone began to overdramatically both ring and vibrate at the same time, breaking the silence and making Snuggles jump and then strive desperately to look cool. Jillian's name flashed up on the screen. Last minute orders, Tabitha assumed.

"Hi Jillian. How are you?" Tabitha answered cheerily.

"Oh Tabitha. It's awful. I don't quite know what to do", came a muffled response. Jillian actually sounded like she might have been crying.

"Jillian, What's happened? Is it Val?" Tabitha felt her tummy lurch.

"No no love. Although dear Val might well have actually lost the plot by now. It's the pitch Tabitha. It's unplayable. It seems that there was more snow last night and it's frozen over what had already frozen over and, oh dear, well I don't think we can get it sorted. I just wanted to give you girls a heads up. If we can't provide the pitch, we forfeit the game and that means..." Jillian sniffed.

"Nil points", Tabitha said slowly. "Oh shit...I mean sorry...bother."

"No problem. It is shit", Jillian responded.

Tabitha took a deep breath and thought. Surely they didn't have any option but to try and get that damn pitch cleared. They had four hours until kick off. She looked out of the window. There was no sign of the sun so nothing was gonna happen naturally.

"Now Jillian. We can do this." Tabitha wasn't sure in the least that they could. "See if you can get any of the other girls down there. With spades or...stuff. Try the ones without kids first I guess. I'll be down there in half an hour. Ok?"

Tabitha got off the phone. She didn't feel anywhere near as calm as she had been trying to sound. She fired off a message to her Mum to let her know the situation. They'd all been planning to come to watch the match later so she wanted to give her warning.

Tabitha couldn't find anything that could potentially be of much help except for a gardening trowel and a broom but she guessed that they would be better than nothing and that every little effort could make a difference. They simply had to try.

Porridge and a sensible meal plan was out of the window now she guessed. She threw some crisps and a pasty into her kit bag and headed out the door. The pavements were starting to thaw nicely already but she guessed that would be from the heat of there being people around. She could only imagine how the playing field would look.

As she walked up it did not look good. It would have been a beautiful scene had it not been for the predicament that they had found themselves in.

Tabitha wandered over to the pitch where Val and Jillian were trying to work some magic with their garden spades. Well they had a clear box at one end at least. Great if it was just a penalty shoot out but she couldn't see how they would make the whole pitch safe in time. They would certainly make sure they could say they'd done their best though.

Tabitha got straight down to work, just focusing on one square foot at a time. If only her watch would go slower. Their progress just wasn't quick enough, even when more of the girls turned up and joined the excavation. Jillian headed backwards and forwards with kettles and urns of hot water.

After an hour Tabitha looked around dismayed. They had made some headway for sure but there was no way that this pitch was gonna pass an inspection. After all, it wasn't the referee's job to take their position in the league into account. Safety was the most important thing and it was their responsibility alone to provide a safe, playable pitch.

If only they had under soil heating like Sonning. There was no doubt that their game would be going ahead, as well as most of the rest of the league who would have had groundsmen or caretakers keeping on top of the situation.

Tabitha saw Jillian look over forlornly and she managed to fake a positive smile despite what was beginning to look like an impossible task.

"We need to take a break ladies", Val called out "or we'll have worse problems to deal with. Please come and grab a hot drink all of you."

The girls all gathered together and gratefully accepted the steaming mugs of hot chocolate on offer.

"Well we can't say we haven't tried." Tabitha put an arm around Jillian who was shivering with both the cold and her dismay.

"I didn't think it would end like this though", Jillian sighed. "I thought we'd at least go down fighting. I'm so gutted for you girls. You've worked so... What the dickens is that noise?"

A loud siren blasted out from the road beyond the trees.

"Whatever it is, it's getting closer." Val called out. "Do we need to find a bloomin' bunker now? Well as if today could get more messed up."

The girls all looked and waited to see what on earth was springing itself upon them now.

The noise got louder and then the source emerged as a big green tractor pulled in through the gates and headed in their direction.

Surely the council couldn't be here to cut the grass. You could hardly see the grass. What on earth was going on? As the tractor became closer though, Tabitha suddenly recognised the grin beneath the safety helmet. Holy moly it was Scott. He must have heard what was going on and come to help them.

Tabitha waved excitedly and ran over to him. The rest of the girls looked on open mouthed. Their hopeless situation now seemed to have acquired a dash of hope.

"Hey Tabby. I heard you might need some assistance", he laughed.

"Well goodness yes, but where did you get, how..?"

"A mate. I fixed the fences on his farm after the wind earlier in the year so he leant me his tractor for our little snow problem. I was after a JCB but you need a different licence for them, so here I am", he laughed.

Yes, here he was, thought Tabitha. She suddenly realised that this was the first time that she'd seen him since 'the dream'. She felt a flush of colour heading up her neck. Oh how times had changed. She liked how he had called it 'our little snow problem' too.

She heard the crunch of footsteps in the snow behind her and Jillian was suddenly there breaking the moment and bringing Tabitha back to reality.

"Hello Ma'am", Scott shouted down. "If you are happy for me to give it a go, I reckon we might be able to find the rest of your pitch down there somewhere."

Jillian beamed. "Young man, you are a hero. Is he your doing Tabitha?"

That sounded rude, thought Tabitha. Oh god, pull it together girl.

"Well I didn't know that he knew, but he's come to try to save the day. This is my friend Scott."

"Scott, I'm delighted to make your acquaintance. Well I guess we'd better get out of your way", she laughed. "Ladies, well done but please move aside", she boomed. "Scott is going to take it from here. Go and get yourselves warmed up."

"Yes", shouted Val joyfully, ushering the girls into the clubhouse. "We have a football match to win."

By the time that the two teams headed out onto the pitch it was completely clear. Friends and family trudged through the snow, looking joyful in the Christmassy scene, some unaware of the potential disaster that the snow had brought with it. Christmas hats and mince pies were shared around and everybody was in great spirits.

Tabitha's Mum jumped up and down, calling out to make sure that Tabitha had seen her. Tabitha waved over, feeling like a five year old in her school nativity play. George and Pam were there and Pam had not broken her promise. There were indeed Pom poms. And there, with his hard hat at his feet, was her friend Scott, her lucky star.

Tabitha felt like the day had already been saved, surrounded by such happiness and festivities, but now it was time to really get down to business and focus on the game. She needed to try to block everything else out. They all needed to. She hoped that the extra pressure of having their loved ones there wouldn't be too much for them.

It wasn't.

They thrived with the support and won 3-2. There was still a chance of survival..maybe.

CHAPTER TWENTY FOUR

A few days later, Tabitha was sitting in a gorgeous little cafe in Paris. Low winter sun shone in through the window. Tabitha shielded her eyes to study her notes.

Andrea and Craig from Yerans were deep in conversation with Frank the director about the vision for the advert...her vision. As Tabitha listened in she still couldn't quite believe that this was really happening and that she was actually here. After all, she recalled, she'd only popped to work at Perfect Promos to sort out their filing and yet, here she was in Paris collaborating with a hugely well known company.

Tomorrow she would be meeting Jean-Pierre, one of the biggest film stars in France and he would be being instructed according to her ideas. It was just crazy.

This was the only work thing that had been set up for today so the rest of the day would be theirs, to take in the sights. Tabitha glanced out of the window. The outside seating area was fully heated so even at this chilly time of year, people were sitting and chatting with friends or quietly just watching the world go by. It was that surreal time between Christmas and New year when many lose track of the days. It was nice to see that some people looked like they may have also allowed themselves the freedom to lose track of the time a little and just appreciate some downtime.

A brass band were setting up across the other side of the square. Tabitha had been to Paris once before and had loved hearing the bands that seemed to be everywhere. It was one of her favourite memories, feeling like she was walking around New Orleans, but a little closer to home. She hoped that these guys would be playing when they left so that they could have a listen.

A mime artist paused to entertain a family that were sitting on a wall nearby. A young child attempted to copy the skills of his new hero before receiving a coin from his Father to put in the entertainer's dish.

Everywhere was so colourful and cheery and Tabitha felt absolutely blissful.

"I love your ideas Tabitha. I think this project will be a lot of fun", Frank nodded approvingly at her.

"Thank you. Thank you so much." Tabitha didn't really know what else to say. She felt like she was in a dream world.

"Right, I'll see you all in the morning. Have a great day." Frank put his papers away into his satchel, passed a handful of notes to the waiter and left them. The waiter came and removed the bill from their table.

"Oh, has he just paid for us too?" asked Tabitha, feeling slightly embarrassed as she put her purse back away.

"It appears so", laughed Craig. "Don't worry, he'll probably be able to claim it back on expenses, the same as we would have done. Anyway, don't you be concerned about things like that. Your ideas are potentially making everybody involved a lot of money so you deserve to have a little cash splashed on you. You are our guest and we won't have you thinking about money..or anything else for that matter. Everything is in hand ok?

"Yes boss", laughed Tabitha. If my orders are just to not worry about anything then I shall simply have to oblige.

From that moment on, Tabitha allowed herself to just completely enjoy her time, as instructed. After all, her part in the project was already completed. It was time to see her plans get put into reality now and just savour the trip.

They spent a fun afternoon visiting the Louvre. Yerans had reserved skip the line tickets for the three of them. Tabitha felt both proud and a little cheeky at the same time as they were shown straight in but once she realised quite how much there was to see, she was very grateful.

The place was amazing, with her personal highlight being the three of them standing in front of the Mona Lisa stating, "It's actually the actual Mona Lisa" repeatedly.

They finished their day with a delicious meal at Le Grand Vefour restaurant. Tabitha was once again blown away when the Maître d' told them that Napoleon and Josephine had regularly frequented the establishment.

When she arrived back at the hotel that evening and phoned her Mum, she was at a loss to know where to even start.

"Start at the very beginning", her Mum sang. Tabitha wasn't quite sure where the song was from but her Mum had often sung it to her and George when they were in a fluster about anything. Tabitha went through every detail of her day excitedly.

"Sounds like you'll sleep well tonight darling. What a day. And tomorrow? Do you get to meet him tomorrow?"

Tabitha was confused for a minute. "Who Mum? Tomorrow they are starting to shoot the advert so I'll be going to the set and..oh, are you talking about Jean-Pierre perchance?"

"Cor blimey, yes of course sweetie."

"Oh I see. I forgot that you liked him", Tabitha teased.

"Really but I did say…"

"Just kidding Mama."

"Well, you know the way you girls all like that Jason Samosa."

"Jason Momoa", Tabitha squealed. "Oh Mum".

"Yes well him, well me and my friends felt the same way about Jean-Pierre Laurent. We didn't have all the social media and online celeb news that you guys have though so we'd watch his films over and over again. Oh and Aunt Cath had a poster of him on her bedroom wall, I remember."

"Well yes, I guess I'll get to see him tomorrow. I'm not sure that I'll meet him though. They'll be far too busy."

"Well darling if you do...."

Her Mother paused. Tabitha wondered what her Mother was going to tell her to do. Mind her manners? Get an autograph? Be friendly?

"Just tell him that I love him", she laughed.

"Ok Mum, cos he won't think that's totally weird or anything. I'll see how it goes. Night Mum."

"Goodnight darling. Sweet dreams."

CHAPTER TWENTY FIVE

As soon as Tabitha walked into the studio the next day with Andrea and Craig, Frank summoned them straight over.

"Guys, welcome. How was your afternoon?" He shook them all by the hand jovially. "We hope you saw a lot of this beautiful city."

"It was fantastic, thank you", Craig enthused. Tabitha and Andrea nodded in agreement whilst both trying not to be too obvious as they stared over Frank's shoulder at Jean-Pierre.

Tabitha could certainly see why her Mum had such a crush on him. He had a real presence about him, even though he was quite a bit older now than the film posters that her Mum had googled and sent to her after their call last night.

Frank followed their gazes and grinned. "Would you like to meet our star Tabitha? We need to make sure that you approve and that he fits with your vision."

Words failed Tabitha but it didn't matter anyway as Frank was already calling over in french to the team. Jean-Pierre swaggered over and Frank spoke more french whilst gesturing towards Tabitha.

Jean-Pierre turned and beamed at her. "Ah, you are the writer", he exclaimed enthusiastically. He shook her hand. "I am loving your work mon chéri."

Tabitha was completely flustered. She didn't know what to say. She had never been great around famous people at the best of times.

She opened her mouth to see what would happen. "Thank you Jean-Pierre. My Mum loves you", she blurted out.

As soon as she had said it, Tabitha prayed that the ground would open up and swallow her. She looked at Andrea and Craig for their help. They must be so horrified. What must Jean-Pierre think of her? This was supposed to be a professional introduction. Oh well, at least she had obeyed her Mum and followed her instructions after all.

Jean-Pierre, it seemed though, was more used to this type of strange behaviour than she gave him credit for and he smiled warmly at her. "Ah well, that is very kind. And I love your mama for sending you to us. This will be much fun."

Remember his exact words Tabitha thought to herself. Mum will want to know his exact words.

"Right", Frank clapped his hands together. "Let's make a start. Guys you are welcome to sit wherever you are comfortable please".

As Jean-Pierre headed back over to make up, Tabitha held her head in her hands. "Oh my god. How awful was that", she laughed.

"Honey it was great", laughed Andrea. "I think it broke the ice nicely".

"I agree", Craig chuckled. "This is supposed to be fun today. Stop beating yourself up. You seem to do the right thing even when you don't think so, ok?"

Tabitha thought about it as they took their seats. Maybe they had a point. Who was to decide what was the right thing to say or do. Maybe sometimes she would say things that were a little wacky but maybe she simply just was a little wacky, and so what.

She was twenty five years old. It was about time that she stopped worrying about what other people thought. She was doing well in life, she had great friends who didn't seem too embarrassed to be around her and her company had been happy to let her represent them many times so it was time to stop right now.

The day was something else. All of the filming team were walking around quoting her lines and Jean-Pierre was perfect for the role. Tabitha hadn't created this advert with a french accent in mind but it added to it perfectly.

"And that's a wrap for today", Frank shouted. "Same time Friday please everybody. Tomorrow I will let you all take a rest so you can have a little celebration of the year tonight."

He headed over to join Tabitha and the Yerans team. "Are you guys happy so far?"

"It's fantastic, thank you", Tabitha exclaimed. "It's more than I could ever have imagined."

"Absolutely what she said", agreed Craig. "I think we're all very happy."

They waved over at Jean-Pierre and the crew as they were about to leave and Jean-Pierre called for them to wait.

"How long is your stay? Will you still be in Paris on Saturday?"

"Yes Sir, we are leaving late on Saturday night". Craig saved Tabitha from trying to speak to Jean-Pierre this time by answering for them all.

"Ah, that is fantastique. I have a box for the Paris St Germain game. Would you like to come…a thank you from me? It will be good huh? Tabitha, do you watch football?"

"That would be great, I do", Tabitha responded "and I also play in a team."

Craig and Andrea looked both shocked and impressed.

Jean-Pierre held his arms aloft in celebration. "You are of many talents Tabitha. Your mama must be a very happy lady."

She certainly would be even happier if she could hear this conversation now.

When they got back to the hotel that night, the three of them headed to the bar for a drink and a wind down. It appeared though that a wind down wasn't the vibe that the hotel was encouraging. They had a lot of international guests staying for New years eve and they had gone to a great effort to ensure that nobody was missing home too much. Champagne and an assortment of canapes were delivered to their table as soon as they sat down and large screens showed firework displays from all around the world. It was a fitting end to an exciting year.

"How did we not know about your football career, I want to hear all about it", Craig probed.

Tabitha laughed. "Well it's not much of a career I'm afraid. It started by accident a few weeks ago and it may well be all over again in a couple of weeks time."

She explained to them about the situation that the team had found itself in. "So I'm afraid we're not quite Paris St Germain. Without investment we won't even be Pa.." she muttered sadly. "But anyway." She didn't want to end the day on a low note. "In the meantime there has been a lot of enjoyment. I absolutely love playing and it just goes to show that it's never too late for a new goal.

"Indeed." Craig nodded.

"Yeah, good for you", Andrea agreed.

CHAPTER
TWENTY SIX

The next couple of days flew by in a flurry of excitement. Filming was a huge success and the three colleagues, now good friends, had made the most of their free time, taking in plenty of what Paris had to offer.

Soon it was their final day in France. It had occurred to Tabitha last night that she could have arranged to catch an earlier flight now that everything was wrapped up so that she could make herself available to play in this afternoon's match but she realised on reflection that it would be very rude to both Yerans and to Jean-Pierre. It had been so kind of him to invite them along to the Paris St Germain game.

Apparently, according to George, it was a clash between the top two teams in the league today and tickets would have been like gold dust. Tabitha's Mother had been quite beside herself with the news of the invitation and also the words that had come out of Jean-Pierre's mouth that he loved her back, even if it was just for providing Tabitha.

She had seconded that it wouldn't be appropriate for Tabitha to come home early but had let her know that she, George and Pam would be going along to cheer on Laura and the team so there would be family representation at the game at least..

Tabitha was awake early. She studied the notes that she had made of the current standings in their league. It was between Woodley and one other team now as to who would be the final unlucky side to be relegated. She had practically discounted next week's final game, with it being against Sonning. Nobody was getting points against them these days. So it seemed that it came down to today. They needed a win. At the very least they needed to better the other team's result. Various connotations began to play out in Tabitha's head. Once she became as involved as looking at goals for and against for both teams, she decided that her time could definitely be better spent.

She climbed out of bed and opened the blinds. It was another cool but sunny day in Paris and it was a terrible shame not to get out and enjoy the morning. She got dressed and headed out through reception. The dining room was being set up for breakfast and the delicious aromas of coffee and pastries spilled out into the foyer.

The doorman nodded and greeted her warmly as she approached. "Good morning Mademoiselle. Is there anything that we can get for you?"

Tabitha felt like she was in a movie. "No, but thank you very much. À plus tard! Merci", she added bravely.

The doorman beamed his approval. "Bien Mademoiselle, très bien."

Tabitha decided that she probably shouldn't go too far away. She still needed to get everything packed up, preferably before their trip to the football. She checked her map and saw that there was a park just ten minutes walk away that would be perfect for some fresh air.

It made a pleasant change to be out and about this early, as the city was just waking. She had thoroughly enjoyed her time in Paris but realised that she hadn't taken much time to herself to just wander around aimlessly.

Tabitha reflected that Paris was a city of both therapeutic relaxation and purposeful rushing about which it managed to combine perfectly. She had never been anywhere else quite like it but somehow it seemed to work. She took in the people sitting outside cafes now, taking their time over their coffee and newspapers as around them waiters scurried about busily preparing for the day ahead. Neither seemed to have any inimical effect on the other. The opposed paces just blended together harmoniously.

As Tabitha arrived at Parc Monceau she immediately realised that this place was much more than she had expected when she had just set out towards the nearest bit of green on her map. A large rotunda stood guard at the entrance of the park, the frost on it's domed roof, beginning to disperse in the morning sun.

For the next hour Tabitha felt as though she had walked into a secret garden although this was possibly even more magical than the film. She headed along beautiful curved walkways that led her to discover all sorts of stunning treasures. Statues would suddenly appear beside the path, where least expected, of celebrated french figures of the arts and there was some amazing architecture including small replicas of an Egyptian pyramid, a Chinese fort, a Dutch windmill and some awesome Corinthian pillars.

Tabitha was grateful that she was able to take some photos or she would hardly have believed what she was seeing herself. The light was stunning now, darting through the branches of the trees. Tabitha could only imagine what this place must look like in full bloom. Maybe she would come back here again one day. Her Mum would absolutely love it.

She sat on a bench to look back through her pictures and just take a moment when she heard a familiar bird above her. She looked up to see if she could catch a glimpse of the noisy woodpecker just as the pecking stopped.

All Tabitha could spot was what looked like a blackbird peering down at her. Then, to her surprise, he turned back to the trunk and began to peck away loudly again. Tabitha put her glasses on to try to get a better view and noticed a splendid red mohican across the bird's head. It appeared that he was enjoying his audience as he stopped and looked down again to make sure that she was still watching before carrying on with his mission.

Tabitha quickly googled and found that what she was witnessing was a black woodpecker. She hadn't even known that they existed. She read on to see that in many ancient cultures they were associated with wishes and luck. Oh, how she hoped that perhaps this could be a good sign for the girls in their football match later.

..And spiritual healing. She looked back up at her new friend to reassure him that she was still paying attention to him at the same time as reading about his super powers. Well she wasn't actually sure that she needed any spiritual healing. Her spirit felt as good as she ever thought it could, potentially the best that it had ever felt.

In fact, thinking about it, everybody was in a pretty good place right now. How marvellous. The world hadn't ended a few months back as she had feared it might do at one sorry point. Instead, everything seemed to be coming together nicely for everyone. Except maybe for Gary. Maybe Gary could still use a little spiritual healing. She'd send it his way. She closed her eyes and wished it on to him.

She wasn't sure why she closed her eyes to do it. Maybe that was just what she learnt as a kid; that magic only worked when you closed your eyes. She smiled as she remembered sitting on the sofa with her Mum and George and chocolate falling from out of the sky if they closed their eyes and wished hard enough. It had been quite a while until she had realised what really happened in those moments and she had been mightily impressed with her Mum for always managing to do a really good throw to get the chocolate bar up high in the air and safely down again without hitting any of them on the bonce.

Tabitha's thoughts were broken as a young child came hurtling around the corner in a little kart. She stopped when she spotted Tabitha sitting on the bench and backpedalled shyly to her parents.

Tabitha supposed that she had better be heading back now anyway. Her suitcase wasn't going to pack itself and she had another exciting adventure to look forward to this afternoon.

Tabitha hadn't quite prepared herself for the amount of attention they received when they arrived at Le Parc de

Princes stadium that afternoon. It was definitely a new experience to be papped alongside a world famous film star but nothing really surprised her for long anymore.

As Jean-Pierre's guests, they were treated to an abundance of fabulous food whilst enjoying an unbeatable view of the pitch. The match was no disappointment either, summed up by Jean-Pierre as a 'spectacle fantastique' which would apparently be talked about for years to come.

Just as she thought the day couldn't have been any more perfect, Tabitha received the text that was the cherry on the icing on the cake. The Woodley girls had won their match. Their relegation rivals had only drawn so survival was back in their hands. But surely they couldn't cause an upset and beat Sonning?

CHAPTER
TWENTY SEVEN

It wasn't long after she was back home from France that Tabitha got to see her teammates and properly congratulate them on their fantastic win. Jillian and Val had decided that a bit of fun was in order before Saturday when the final match would be upon them.

Nearly End of Season party! the text had announced. *Tuesday at the clubhouse 7-11pm. Not too much drinking maybe on a 'school night' but bring a bottle if you please. All supporters and little ones are welcome along! The more the merrier. Let's celebrate making it to the end of the season in one piece :-) x*

As much as Tabitha was excited to see everybody in a more relaxed situation she was also sadly aware that this had probably been arranged because Jillian and Val didn't think that they stood a chance of winning on Saturday.

They obviously wanted them all to have a fun event together before they had to face the sadness of it all coming to an end.

Pam tried to gee her up and suggested that maybe it was just a last minute team building exercise but Tabitha wasn't convinced. Jillian and Val knew most of the girls well that they would be playing on Saturday. They knew what they were going to be facing.

Still, a party was a party and once Tuesday actually arrived and the group were all together, they quickly all realised that they did have something very special to celebrate. Jeez, half of them had hardly kicked a football before and somehow they had managed to form a team that played pretty well together and had even won some games. What an achievement. Whatever happened beyond Saturday, they would certainly remember this exciting time of their lives with pride and great fondness.

Tabitha's Mum and Pam had come along with her to the party and George and Scott were joining them later after they'd finished a job. Tabitha had told them all that they didn't need to feel obliged but her nearest and dearest weren't ones to turn down a shindig.

It was funny to see all of the girls glammed up for a change. They were used to seeing each other out in their trackies and baggy t-shirts. They didn't look like the same muddy, sweaty girls from that first training session. As well as their dressy and laundered clothes and styled hair this evening, every one of them seemed to wear an extra layer of confidence after what they had been a part of.

Val danced over to their group and gave Tabitha a hug. "Isn't this lovely dear?", she shouted over the music. "I do hope your fella is coming along later. We probably wouldn't have gotten this far without him and his tractor."

Tabitha felt herself blush. "Oh Val, he's not my fella", she laughed "but yes, he'll be here in a bit."

Val gave her a knowing look and a wink and danced away.

Oh god, thought Tabitha. If Val could tell that she had turned peculiar about Scott then did that mean that he could tell too? How embarrassing. And her brother would completely disown her.

She didn't have too much time to worry about that now as Jillian clapped her hands and tapped on a microphone to get everybody's attention. Tabitha wondered since when did Jillian need a microphone to be heard but it all became clear as she announced that there was a karaoke machine in the building.

"So don't be shy my darlings. Me and Val are gonna show you how it's done but I would like names and songs on papers in this bucket quick sharp please.

A lot of the girls looked as wide eyed and nervous now as when they had first met 'Jill' but she and Val didn't hold back in getting things started as they led the whole room in a fantastic rendition of Sweet Caroline.

When they had finished they looked in the still empty bucket.

"Right then ladies, it's gonna be like that is it", laughed Val. "Ok you spoilsports, unless you want to hear us sing all night we'd best be seeing some names and songs soon pleeeease." She looked around desperately.

Jillian was not going to see her friend's fun idea go to waste. "Ladies", she boomed. "You can choose what to sing or I will choose for you. I am still your gaffer till Saturday." She couldn't help but laugh but her words were enough to make everybody realise that actually they needed to step up. Every one of them looked around the room to see who would be brave enough to volunteer first.

"Aha, I know how we could begin", Jillian continued now that she very much had everyone's attention. She looked around the room for her chosen prey. "Tabitha."

Tabitha froze as all eyes turned to her. Oh crikey, Tabitha thought. Had she really said her name. Why oh why? Her teammates looked both sorry for her but thankful at the same time that they were free, for now.

"Our dear Tabitha", Jillian continued. "Do you remember our first meeting?"

"Uh yes, of course", Tabitha stammered.

"Mmm", Jillian started to pace up and down now, enjoying being in character. "I seem to remember you....chatting....to Laura whilst it was not your turn to chat. Do you remember that Tabitha?" Jillian had to look away as she struggled to keep a straight face.

"Oh yes". Tabitha grinned as she felt, once again, as if she was back at school.

"Well why don't you come up and get us started? As we do actually love you now, you can choose your own song though. Deal?"

The room was filled with a tense silence and then everybody burst into applause as Tabitha nodded and headed to the microphone. There was no way that she was getting out of this so she may as well get it over and done with.

She looked down the song list which looked slightly blurry due to her nerves and her second gin and tonic.

Ah, that could work. Lucky Star. She'd been singing that song for days anyway. Actually, since the day of Scott and the tractor, when he'd been her lucky star. This would be a good choice as everyone would know at least some of the words hopefully, and well, she had to sing something and quickly before the pressure built even more.

As the intro started, there was a cheer and Tabitha was grateful that it did indeed look like she would have some accompaniment from the girls.

She had a great laugh once she got into it, even pulling out a few of Madonna's dance moves from the video and the other girls gradually began to wander up and place their song choices into the bucket. It occurred to Tabitha that their new found keenness was a little insulting as it meant they were happy to follow her but, hey ho, it was all good fun.

By the time that the song finished, Tabitha was almost disappointed to have to step away from the microphone which, she decided, probably meant that it was good that she had to.

She skipped through the huddle of what she now liked to think of as her fans, back to the safety of her Mum and Pam. She came back to earth as she saw that her brother had arrived while she was singing and he was just grinning broadly at her. Here we go, she thought as she waited for his critique. He stroked his chin in true Simon Cowell fashion then took a sharp intake of breath.

"You know what sis", he nodded his head thoughtfully then laughed. "That wasn't awful."

Tabitha decided that she'd take that and she gratefully took her drink back from Pam.

As she took a relieved sip, she felt a hand placed firmly on her lower back and turned to see Scott standing there behind her. "That was great Tabby. You have got some balls, girl", he laughed.

"Thanks. Hi", she replied, thinking that she could do with swapping her 'balls' for a steadier pair of legs right at this moment.

Thankfully everybody's attention turned back to the front of the room as the next song began.

Tabitha tried her best to regain her composure. Act normal, she thought as she caught her Mum's eye. She could tell by her Mum's face that she had sussed her out. Great!

CHAPTER TWENTY EIGHT

Tabitha had watched Living with Lions once with her brother. Huge, brave rugby players out on tour, were running to be sick before going onto the pitch to play a game that they were great at and loved. She hadn't really understood how they got quite so wound up over what was just sport.

Today she understood!

She felt like she'd had about six minutes sleep although she remembered dreaming a couple of times so was sure that she must have had more.

Food wasn't pleasurable today. She felt like a machine, just putting in fuel. That was certainly not the relationship that she liked to have with food. Bugger the food is fuel malarky. Food or 'nom noms' is yummy was usually more her philosophy, even when dieting.

Today was different though. It was match day. The match day. She'd attended many match days. A fun day out with her friends watching Reading, grabbing a burger afterwards but now match day was something completely different altogether.

The team stood in a circle in their changing room, their arms around each other's shoulders forming a dedicated bond. Jillian and Val stood on the periphery. The time for instructions and orders was over and they spoke calmly about pride and enjoyment and composure.

Tabitha looked around the circle at her teammates and thought back to that first day when they had come together. Only a few weeks ago most of them didn't even know each other. She told herself that really there was nothing to lose and everything to gain today. She didn't believe herself for one minute but this was going to be her mantra so that she could enjoy the occasion.

"Let's go ladies please", the referee called at the door.

The crowd whooped and hollered their support as they headed out onto the pitch and took their formation. Then all eyes turned back to the door as they awaited their competition. Tabitha felt like she was in a Royal rumble waiting to see which WWF superstar was coming out to fight next. As a tense silence spread around the team she half expected to hear the Undertaker's music float across the field.

Sonning suddenly burst through the doors with an energy more reminiscent of the Ultimate Warrior. They all ran out in a perfectly formed line, standing tall and looking fit. It occurred to Tabitha that they may as well have beaten their chests as they arrived on the pitch. There definitely would have been some standing and shaking of the ropes, had they actually been in a wrestling ring.

Val and Jillian smiled politely to a few of their old girls that looked their way as they passed by them, but their personal hurt was clear to see. It spurred Tabitha on more. How could these lot do the dirty on two such nice, dedicated ladies? It wasn't like they had left to get paid a fortune in a top Premier league club. They just had a bit of food provided and got their kits washed after matches. They'd been easily bought. These were not the type of people that Tabitha was going to bow down to easily.

She eyed the girl that would be defending her and told herself that she could match her. These lot were great as a team, of course, but all she could do was nullify her counterpart. The whistle blew and the game began.

For the first few minutes it felt like Sonning were just toying with them as they passed the ball between themselves. Tabitha felt like a piggy in the middle, arriving to tackle the opposition just as they offloaded the ball to the next player. It got to a point where she would have felt less embarrassed if they would at least shoot at goal.

She guessed that they were just trying to build up their possession stats to show their dominance.

They hardly needed to waste time doing that though, thought Tabitha. Everybody was aware of their dominance. They were definitely winning this league, whatever the score today.

One of Woodley's defenders eventually got impatient and maybe a little humiliated with their display and went in for a tackle. She won the ball cleanly but the Sonning player hopped around, claiming that she had been hurt terribly. The referee blew his whistle for a free kick for Sonning and the, not so injured, player smiled her appreciation and stepped up to take the shot.

Ok it was going to be like that was it, Tabitha thought. She looked over to the bench where Jillian looked rather woeful already. Right, this was not happening on her watch. 'Game on bitches', she said in her head and pulled her shoulders back.

Sonning's shot at goal was slightly wide but surely it would only be a matter of time.

When the game restarted, Tabitha managed to beat her opposite number to the ball. She dribbled down the left side of the pitch whilst looking to see what was on. Her teammates watched her and then continued watching her. Oh crikey, somebody needed to make themselves available. She pointed out to her centre forward where she was going to put the ball through and thankfully she ran on to it. Two more successful passes and they forced a save from the keeper and they were in the game.

Woodley's energy changed immediately. Whatever the end result, this could be the last game they all ever played together and so play, they would.

The more that they got into the game, the louder the crowd got. Tabitha even managed a chuckle at her Mum and Pam shaking their pom poms (or pam pams as they had renamed them) and calling out an inaudible chant. She spotted her friends from work in the crowd and gave them a sneaky wave when she got a chance. Peter waved a vape at her proudly. Tabitha was thrilled he was trying to get off the cigs at last but maybe she would wait till later to congratulate him.

Their defence worked so hard, repelling attack after attack and somehow, with just two minutes until halftime, the game was still goalless.

Maybe Sonning had underestimated them and not brought their A game or maybe Woodley had become a pretty decent team themselves after all. They had been so poor when they were first put together that Tabitha had known that they could only improve week by week but this felt as though they had been playing together as a unit for years.

Just as Tabitha was revelling in a newly found confidence, Sonning sent in a ball from what seemed like about 30 yards outside of their box. Their goalkeeper dove desperately to save it but it was hammered into the top right corner of the net.

Tabitha was gutted. It was so close to halftime and Sonning had broken the duck. Woodley's heads dropped as they realised that the inevitable was surely about to happen now. The whole crowd went eerily quiet after the initial celebration from Sonning's friends and family. Even they now looked a little sorry for Woodley which just made it all even sadder.

The teams headed back into their positions for the restart.

Val jumped up and shouted from the sideline. "Keep your heads, my girls. Let's get to halftime."

Even though it was common sense, it was the words that were needed as Woodley got back stuck in to protecting their goal. They ended the half with nine players behind the ball but sometimes needs must and when the half time whistle blew, the damage remained at a one goal deficit.

The girls sat in the changing rooms with wide eyes, a mixture of adrenaline and exhaustion surging through even the more established players in the team.

"Darlings you were great", Jillian enthused. "Brave, Strong, Determined. I'm so proud of you all. I hope that you are too."

The common response was a kind of 'meh'.

"Now come on", Val shook her fist. "We are in this game. Some people wouldn't have given us a hope but we still have a chance. Let's think of some of the drills we did on Thursday once we're back out there. See the lines that you want to play and put yourselves in the positions to do it." " Well, when they allow us possession", she added, a little quieter.

"And another thing ladies, get into those tackles. If they get a free kick, so be it, they're hogging possession anyway so we might as well give it a go and try to steal some more ball."

She had a point, thought Tabitha. They couldn't give away possession that they didn't have. Just territory, and most of the play was already in their half anyway. Yes, attack was the new defence she thought and felt a renewed energy in her.

As they stood to head back out, they all looked fired up again after the halftime team talk and the excited buzz was back.

"Oh, one last thing, don't get sent off, hey ladies. This referee ain't giving us anything", shouted Val.

They headed back out to the pitch where Sonning were waiting for them, having come out first. Tabitha preferred this. It was Woodley's turn to make a grand entrance and try to look intimidating. She called to the crowd for their best cheer as they ran out.

"Come on", she shouted and stared fiercely at her opposition. This half they were going to take control. These Sonning girls had had a lot go their way this season. Now they were gonna see what a real battle was about.

Two minutes later Woodley were 2-0 down.

CHAPTER TWENTY NINE

When Tabitha had been small she had always wanted to be able to do what her brother could do. He could reach things that she couldn't. He could run faster than her. She was constantly watching and learning and striving for her next goal. Each time that she had achieved what she'd dreamt of, she was already focussing on the next thing, so she never really celebrated her successes as she should have.

Finally, when she was ten she began to feel satisfied with her achievements. She was good at both skipping and marbles and did well in her school lessons too. At last she had felt accomplished without comparing herself to other people.

Then she'd had to go to big school and start all over again from the bottom. Once again she would look at the older people. They were so tall and had pierced ears and even though they did have to cover their earrings with plasters, they looked so cool. She couldn't wait to be like them. Surely it must feel like being in the movie Grease constantly.

However, when she got to their age, she soon realised that there was a lot going on behind the scenes. Sure, she could wear an inch heel on her court shoes and put half a can of hairspray on her fringe each day (she would forever send apologies to the ozone layer) but there was suddenly the feeling of wanting everything to just slow down a bit.

Now there was a real apprehension of what would happen next. Where would she get a job? Had she and her friends chosen the right options and would they ever see each other again once they left school?

For the first time ever she had wanted to freeze time instead of pushing ahead with getting older and taller and faster. It was a glorious feeling in a way as it made her realise that she was completely happy where she was right now and that was partly why she didn't want anything to change. From that time forward she had learnt to embrace every moment.

Even looking forward to something exciting had a new meaning. She wouldn't pine for an event to arrive anymore. She would enjoy the anticipation of it as much as it happening sometimes and then once it was over she would cherish the memory. Life was so much better without emotional comedowns after pinning all her thoughts on one party and then it being over.

Each day was there to be lived. There was nothing that couldn't be fixed and there were many new adventures and feelings still to be discovered. It made life so much better once she had discovered these freedoms.

Some days would still be harder than others of course but even then, lessons would be learnt from those days. There was so much truth in the words of the song, Que sera sera. Whatever came along to challenge her, there would always be hope....

CHAPTER THIRTY

At 2-0 down it was time to reassess what they were going to get out of this game. They certainly didn't want to get humiliated with a hiding but they had not worked this hard to now just sit back and defend for another forty minutes either. They just had to pull their socks up and go again.

It appeared that Tabitha's opposite number thought that the game was won already though as Tabitha won possession a little too easily, in her opinion only. She then skilfully kicked the ball past her nemesis and ran back on to it. She crossed the ball into the box beautifully and….SCORE!

Woodley's striker who was about a foot and a half shorter than the Sonning defender headed the ball into the goal, almost under her armpit. It was a total David and Goliath moment and it was game on. The Sonning team all looked to the referee but there was no issue at all with the goal and everybody retook their places.

"Go on Woodley", shouted George. Tabitha looked over to her family proudly. It was a lovely surprise to see Andrea and Craig from Yerans standing there too with Lizzie and the office gang. She had talked to them about her football briefly while they were in Paris of course but how kind that they had taken the time to come and support her. She felt rude that she couldn't go over and say hello and introduce them to everybody.

Her mind was brought back to the pitch in a haste as her opposite number got the ball and began to hurtle down her wing. Tabitha reacted too late and caught her heel clumsily.

The referee pulled out his first yellow card of the afternoon. Feeling gutted, Tabitha bit her lip and waved an apology to her team as Sonning lined up the free kick. Tabitha knew that there was no time to dwell on it now. She needed to refocus quickly and as Sonning went to take a short free kick, she ran and intercepted the ball and kicked it out of play, via their player, giving Woodley possession back.

They held onto it for a bit, passing the ball in triangles as they had practised so often, gradually tempting the

Sonning players out of their defence as they began to get frustrated. Suddenly it felt as though the match had gone into slow motion as Woodley's left back spotted a gap that had been created and fired the ball through.

'Go on, go on hon'. Tabitha willed Laura to get to the shot. She did. She controlled the ball under her foot, then shimmied past her defender and then slotted the ball into the net stunningly. Laura jumped up and down in surprise and then ran over to Martin and the children. Martin only just managed not to drop their youngest with the excitement and Laura was gleefully mobbed by them all. The crowd had gone crazy now. It was like the team had just won the fa cup. Somehow they were back level. In fact, thought Tabitha, it wasn't somehow. It was deserved.

Everybody was brought back to earth as the referee blew on his whistle sharply and gave Laura a yellow card for over celebrating.

"Oh you…..!" Thankfully the whistle blew again to block out Val's reaction to the pernickety referee and calm was eventually restored.

Both teams went back into their positions for the restart.

Sonning looked a little nervous now. It occurred to Tabitha that often when a team was used to winning, they weren't always quick to find a plan B when things weren't working out as they'd expected. This spurred her on even more and she got the better of her opposition once again.

The pass was on to a teammate but she also had a clear sight at goal. Maybe she had a better chance than her teammate. Or maybe she should pass. Or. Jeez, there was no time to analyse now for heaven's sake, she realised as she was getting closed down. Two defenders had completely blocked the pass now so there was no option left but to shoot. She focused on the goal. She put her foot through the ball and held her breath.

If Tabitha had been playing rugby that day it would have been quite a score but she wasn't. She held her head in her hands as the ball flew way over the goal and off into the distance. That could be it. Surely there couldn't be much time left. Tabitha was distraught.

As the ball was retrieved by the crowd, rain began to drizzle down onto the players. It felt like a terribly sad way for it all to end. Tabitha walked back up the pitch with her head down. A tear snuck down her cheek, thankfully hidden by the raindrops.

As the Sonning goalkeeper went to restart the game, the crowd came back to life as Jillian jumped up and waved her arms about, encouraging one final wave of support for her brave girls.

Tabitha looked over at her loved ones through the rain. They didn't look disappointed. They didn't care that they were getting wet. They were huddled together and laughing and still singing loudly. Tabitha's mind went back to the evening that she had trained with George and Scott. The night when she had realised that she could actually kick a ball. Her brother's words from that night echoed around her mind.

"Never hang your head. If you make a howler and need to react, you look to the sky, not the floor alright. Head up."

Tabitha flinched against the rain as she looked up into the sky. Apart from mentally making her feel stronger, her breath was fuller as her neck lengthened. She took a couple more deep breaths and then fixed her attention back to the game.

The referee looked at his watch. This action spurred the crowd on again and as Woodley managed to win the ball in their own half, they were willed forward by what now looked and sounded like most of the neighbourhood.

The girls all knew that they were running out of time and chances but the focus on their faces showed that they were not going to bow out without one more fight.

Pass after pass was completed with astounding precision.

It was suddenly as if they were magnets, drawing the ball to their feet. Sonning just couldn't get to them in time. The play gradually moved up the pitch. The referee looked at his watch again but they were through. Surely Woodley would get one last shot. Tabitha ran towards the box to offer her support and took an unfriendly elbow to the chin for her trouble. As she struggled to stay on her feet the whistle blew. The referee must have seen the elbow. They'd have a free kick.

But nobody was looking in her direction. Her heart sank. It must have been the whistle for full time she concluded, rubbing her jaw as everything seemed to go a little slower around her. Oh goodness, she felt like she might be going down. The team was going down and it seemed that, thanks to her last encounter, so was she.

The crowd erupted with cheers and applause as she collapsed to her knees. She raised her head and through the blurriness managed to make out her teammates. Her teammates that were lifting one of their players into the air. What the? Holy Cow. Could it be....? Yeeesss! Woodley had scored. That was why the whistle had been blown.

"We scored", Tabitha repeated over and over again as she was helped from the pitch.

"And we've won darling", Jillian squealed delightedly. "It's all over."

"Oh", Tabitha tried to go back to her team.

"You might need to sit for just a minute hon. You got quite a knock but don't worry. There'll be plenty of time to celebrate. We'll sort you out an ice pack."

"Oh", Tabitha looked over to the team and the supporters. Everybody was jumping around in the rain. With the grogginess from the knock on her chin, everything had a surreal feeling about it. The fact that everything was in slow motion meant that she just had longer to capture the memory.

Her Mother arrived beside her and hugged her tightly just as she was wondering why Craig and Andrea were shaking hands with Jillian.

CHAPTER
THIRTY ONE

So sometimes in life, two worlds collide. Tabitha was always a firm believer in fate and the fact that anything was possible. However, she still couldn't quite get her head around the fact that two of her own worlds had collided yesterday.

She'd had to question if she was actually concussed as Val had announced to the team after the match that Yerans had offered, no, requested to provide them with sponsorship next season.

After all, Andrea had explained, Yerans was all about eating healthy but easy food whilst on the run. What better than a women's football team to carry their name and to appear in one of their adverts. It was an ideal partnership and it meant that the team would actually survive.

After the madness of the day, the silence had been deafening when Tabitha laid in bed later that night. Everything had come together so perfectly but there was just one thing that was still troubling her. She had agreed to go to the races the next day with George and Pam but the fact that Scott was going to be there had given her butterflies. She didn't know how she was going to get him out of her system. It wasn't like he or she were going anywhere soon. He was always going to be around and he would be so freaked out if he knew how she was feeling.

She flicked on the tv and found an old black and white movie. The sound was down but it was easy to see that it was probably near the delightful end. A handsome man gazed into the face of a doe eyed girl. Her eyes were teary from the love that she obviously felt for him. He gently lifted her chin and kissed her full on the lips. Tabitha swooned and turned it back off, eventually falling into a restless sleep.

CHAPTER THIRTY TWO

Tabitha eventually managed to hide her bruised chin with some expertly applied foundation the next morning. She was damned if she was going to wear a nice dress to the horse racing, only to look like a thug that had been caught up in a fight the night before.

"So are you ready to have a little splutter today then Tabs", laughed George as they arrived.

"Ha ha. How come your memory is suddenly so good, hey?" she joshed back.

"Now now kids, play nice", Scott laughed, putting an arm around each of their backs to separate them and guide them through to the betting ring.

"I know now that it's called a flutter", she rolled her eyes playfully to Pam. "So do you have any idea who you're betting on hon?" Tabitha looked to see if there were any names that sprung out to her.

"George says that Trojan jr. is a good bet for the 3:15. Him and Scott have been enthusing about that horse all season. Today could be a big day for him."

"Trojan jr.", Tabitha giggled. That sounds like a type of condo..."

"Dude", shouted George.

"Oops sorry bro", Tabitha laughed. "Anyway we'd better get on with it or we'll miss the starting barrier".

"Gate!" the other three shouted in unison.

"Maybe you should stick to football babe", Pam chortled.

They all laughed all afternoon and Tabitha could see why the boys enjoyed coming along to the racing. The atmosphere was electric.

Her betting had been far from successful but she decided that maybe it was somebody else's turn to have some luck. She had been receiving it by the bucketload recently.

Soon it was time for the race that she was confident about though, thanks to now having heard about Trojan jr.

for nearly two hours. He was a beautiful looking horse to be fair but she didn't need to know every detail about his breeding, his training as a yearling or his best suited jockey.

It was really cool to see George and Scott so animated though as the horses lined up. Fairplay, they had been this animated for her yesterday. In fact they supported all of her stuff so she was certainly excited to get into this with them now.

As the runners and riders were called out, Tabitha was amazed to hear that there was a horse in the race called Lucky Star. How on earth had she missed that? She would definitely have put her money on him.

"Did I hear that right?" she asked Pam.

"Oh yeah hon. Didn't you see? He's not actually that bad for a relative newbie."

Tabitha was a little disappointed but she'd look out for him next time. At least she could give all of her backing and attention to Trojan jr. right now and if he won this race she would be involved in a bit of history in the record books apparently.

It looked very much like she had finally bet on the right horse as Trojan jr. took an early lead. It sounded as though most of the stand had bet on him too as the cheers got louder as the race went on.

One more lap and she'd actually make a bit of money back. Maybe she should have put more on him. After all he was a hot tip but...oh wait....Trojan jr. was being closed down.

Tabitha wished that she had brought her glasses as she strained to see what was going on over the other side of the racetrack. As the front pack came nearer, she could see that Trojan jr. was being chased closely by the horse with the jockey with the orange spotted hat. She flicked her programme open.

Oh, well this could be a reflection of her usual gambling luck.

It was Lucky Star hurtling forward to try to spoil the party. The frenzied shouts got louder in the stand as the horses rounded the bend and ran past them again. Trojan jr. and Lucky star were neck and neck now. They looked like they were both having the time of their lives, unaware of the responsibility of their run, just having a nice little play together.

As they ran towards the finishing line, all the heads in the crowd simultaneously switched from watching the track to the tv, to the track, to the tv. The voice on the tannoy got faster and louder until "And Lucky Star has it. Lucky Star takes the win. Trojan jr is a close 2nd".

There were a few cheers from people who had backed the right horse then the crowd went on about their business of heading to the bars or getting a bet on the next race.

"Oh well" exclaimed George. "You win some, you lose some but jeez that was close." He and Pam tore up their betting slips and headed off towards the bar arm in arm.

Tabitha looked down to see who she had in the next race. "Well Scott. It's a shame Trojan jr. didn't get the record but this makes the next meeting exciting hey?"

She looked at Scott for a response to find him just grinning at her.

"What? Did I say something silly again? I meant, you know, I mean, now that there's a new competitor in the field it'll be exciting, hey?"

Scott continued to smile. Now she was starting to feel quite perturbed.

"What is it Scott? Do I have something on my face? Are you actually ok?"

Scott finally found his words. "I won Tabby. I won big. I didn't bet on Trojan jr. I bet on Lucky Star. He took a deep breath and looked serious now. "I bet on Lucky Star Tabitha because I remembered you singing that song."

Tabitha caught her breath and swallowed hard. Maybe she could actually come clean after all and admit that he had been the inspiration behind her song choice that night but oh god, what if he never spoke to her again. She couldn't stand that.

She opened her mouth to just say something, anything at the same time as Scott took hold of both of her hands and looked intently into her eyes.

The whole world around them disappeared

"And furthermore Tabby, the more time I spend around you, the more I win big. I apologise for any inconvenience but I'm afraid that I'm in love with you Tabitha Morris. You are my lucky star."

Tabitha couldn't believe what she was hearing. After all this time and fretting, could he really actually feel the same way as she did?

"What? I mean, am I actually?" she gasped. "But no. You're mine. That's why I chose...."

She was sure that she literally swooned at that moment as she felt as though her knees might actually buckle beneath her. Just in time he gently pulled her into his arms.

His eyes sought her permission and she nodded assuredly as she raised her face to meet his kiss. The first kiss, it transpired, of many.

Printed in Great Britain
by Amazon

80664358R00149